MW00509445

THE WEDDING DRIVER

LOVE IN THE ADIRONDACKS

JEN TALTY

JUPITER PRESS

THE WEDDING DRIVER

LOVE IN THE ADIRONDACKS, BOOK 3

USA Today Bestseller
JEN TALTY

PRAISE FOR JEN TALTY

"Deadly Secrets is the best of romance and suspense in one hot read!" *NYT Bestselling Author Jennifer Probst*

"A charming setting and a steamy couple heat up the pages in a suspenseful story I couldn't put down!" *NY Times and USA today Bestselling Author Donna Grant*

"Jen Talty's books will grab your attention and pull you into a world of relatable characters, strong personalities, humor, and believable storylines. You'll laugh, you'll cry, and you'll rush to get the next book she releases!" Natalie Ann USA Today Bestselling Author

"I positively loved *In Two Weeks*, and highly recommend it. The writing is wonderful, the story is fantastic, and the characters will keep you coming back for more. I can't wait to get my hands on future installments of the NYS Troopers series." *Long and Short Reviews*

"In Two Weeks hooks the reader from page one. This is a fast paced story where the develop-

ment of the romance grabs you emotionally and the suspense keeps you sitting on the edge of your chair. Great characters, great writing, and a believable plot that can be a warning to all of us." *Desiree Holt, USA Today Bestseller*

"*Dark Water* delivers an engaging portrait of wounded hearts as the memorable characters take you on a healing journey of love. A mysterious death brings danger and intrigue into the drama, while sultry passions brew into a believable plot that melts the reader's heart. Jen Talty pens an entertaining romance that grips the heart as the colorful and dangerous story unfolds into a chilling ending." *Night Owl Reviews*

"This is not the typical love story, nor is it the typical mystery. The characters are well rounded and interesting." *You Gotta Read Reviews*

"*Murder in Paradise Bay* is a fast-paced romantic thriller with plenty of twists and turns to keep you guessing until the end. You won't want to miss this one..." *USA Today bestselling author Janice Maynard*

BOOK DESCRIPTION

Love in the Adirondacks—where hearts come together like the moon and the stars shining bright in the sky, showing the boats the way home at night.

The Wedding Driver: He's been making dreams come true for a decade. Never in a million years did he believe his dream was a boat ride away.

Tonya Johnson has been in love with the elusive Foster Landon for as long as she can remember. However, other than their mutual business arrangement of her wedding planning business and the fact that he takes newlyweds around the bay on his antique boat shortly after their nuptials, he barely gives her the time of the day. Well, she's tired of being ignored and decides it's time Foster Landon takes her out on a proper date.

Foster Landon had his heart broken once and he doesn't plan on letting that happen again. While he believes in love, it's not for him. Not anymore. That is until Tonya asked him to take him for a boat ride. And not a wedding ride. He should say no, but he couldn't resist her smile. Besides, of all the wedding planners in the area, she brought him the most business. Who was he to say no? However, he wasn't prepared to lose his heart and find himself wanting to become a groom.

To Valerie Vandette. Thanks for the all the childhood memories on Cleverdale! Your friendship has always meant a lot to me! And to Jon Kaplan. The original Wedding Driver. Thanks for the idea!

onya Johnson took the line that Foster Landon tossed and secured the old wooden boat with the name *The Wedding Driver* proudly displayed on the stern.

"Are you ready for tomorrow?" Foster asked as he jumped onto the dock. Weddings always put him in a good mood. Odd for someone who had sworn off romance for the rest of his life.

"I'm not the one getting married." She glanced over her shoulder. The sun had disappeared behind the mountains, casting a fiery glow over Lake George. She'd lived here her entire life, and she couldn't imagine being anywhere else.

Except maybe in Foster's arms.

"Someday, some man is going to swoop in and sweep you off your feet." Foster offered her a helping hand as they navigated the stairs toward his house, which needed a lot of work. Well, not according to Foster. It was fine for his needs.

That wasn't a false statement.

"You should know me better by now that I don't want that." She didn't want any member of the opposite sex to come in and romance her like she was some prize. For a couple of years, she'd known exactly what she wanted in a man, and he had a name. All she had to do was get the courage to ask him out.

He chuckled. "Would you like to stay and have a drink? Maybe catch up on that show we've been watching. I believe another episode dropped. Or do you have family obligations with your sister's wedding?"

"They have the best wedding planner ever. It's all taken care of. As long as the wedding driver shows up on time, it's all good."

He poked her biceps before opening the door.

Sometimes the way Foster behaved felt like flirting. However, he never carried it further. His gazes often lasted longer than they should, but not so long she could consider them an invitation. He always treated her with respect. He did things like open doors for her and take her elbow when she was in high heels and needed to navigate rough terrain while working a wedding where he was contracted to be the wedding driver, which was as many as she could talk the couples into.

"You're never going to let me live down being late that one time."

"Nope. Never." She smiled. "Do you have popcorn?"

"I also stocked up on hot chocolate and marshmallows."

"Oh. Well, I'm not leaving now." Her sisters both thought she was crazy. Foster spent his time dealing with his ex-wife and mourning the death of his daughter. According to Tayla, Foster was emotionally unavailable. That because he continually chose to live in the past while Tonya was standing right in front of him, he'd never make that giant leap.

Her grandfather had a different opinion, only his required her to do something.

"Why don't you make yourself comfortable? I'll get our snack." Foster winked.

She plopped down on the big brown leather sofa, tucking her feet under her butt and wrapping herself in a soft fleece blanket. Her cell buzzed. She pulled it out of her back pocket.

The bride.

"Are you panicking?" Tonya didn't bother to say hello.

"No. Yes. I don't know," Tiki said. "This wedding has turned into more than I expected."

Tonya bit her tongue. Saying *I told you so* wouldn't be too smart right about now. She'd been planning weddings since before she graduated college. She only finished her education because her parents and grandpa would have flipped out if she hadn't. However, her business had become successful her sophomore year and has continued to grow.

"What's concerning you right now?"

"Want to come over? Or I can come to you?"

"I'm not home yet." Tonya sighed. She'd given up many nights with Foster for her family or because of his ex-wife. Not that it mattered. She should be scrolling through the dating app that she'd downloaded again but hadn't re-registered her account. She'd decided that she was finally going to ask out Foster.

Again.

"Where are you?" Tiki asked.

"Foster and I just finished a wedding."

"I see," Tiki said.

"Look. Trust me. I've taken care of everything. You and Lake are going to have a great wedding. I promise."

"I know. I'm just being a nervous bride. I want everything to be perfect, especially since it's not in New York City and the Grant's family country club."

"Oh. That's what this is about." Tonya tucked the cell under her ear as she took the mug of cocoa and mouthed *Tiki* to Foster.

He sat down in the recliner.

Tonya's heart dropped to her pinky toe. He rarely shared the sofa, but she always hoped he would.

"Stop worrying about it. Lake didn't want it there. His sister backed him up and both his parents eventually came on board," Tonya said.

"It's the eventually part that has me stressing."

"Do you need to go?" Foster whispered as he set the popcorn bowl between them on the small end table.

"Where's Lake?"

"He's in the kitchen chatting with his parents and his sister. Twice the country club came up. I'd call Tayla, but Mom has her doing all sorts of shit."

"Why don't you meet me at my place in fifteen."

"Are you sure?"

"I wouldn't offer if I didn't mean it." Tonya sighed, setting her hot chocolate down. She stood. "I'm leaving in five." She ended the call. "I'll have to take a rain check."

"I totally understand." He took her by the hand and led her to the front door. "I'll see you tomorrow."

"Why don't we go together? You'll need help with the boat."

He lowered his chin. "You have bridesmaid things to do. I can handle this one on my own." He leaned in and kissed her cheek. His warm, sweet lips lingered for a long, torturous moment.

She thought about grabbing his shoulders and kissing him, hard. However, she didn't have the courage.

Tomorrow, when the mood was romantic and the time was right, she'd ask him out on a real date.

Shit. She was the queen of procrastination.

Foster took the plastic bags filled with food and water and made his way down one alleyway after the other, doing his best to put Tonya out of his mind.

For seven years he'd lived without sex and it hadn't been that hard. Only, nothing was simple anymore when it came to Tonya. His feelings were all over the place and he couldn't trust that he could keep a lid on his desires. He shouldn't have invited her to stay earlier, so when she left, part of him had been relieved.

While the other part had been more than disappointed.

As long as he continued to keep Tonya in the friend zone, his life should continue on the same path. That's the way he wanted it. Needed it. Complicating his relationship with Tonya would be disastrous. He couldn't go down that road. Thinking about it hurt his soul in ways he couldn't describe.

But mostly he didn't want to hurt Tonya. The only problem was he could feel things shifting and her emotions were pulling him closer. If she acted on them, he had no idea if he could shut them down.

"Excuse me. Tony, right?" Foster approached a familiar man sitting on a couple of old milk crates.

"Foster." Tony nodded. "How are you?" He smiled, showing off the eight teeth he had remaining.

"I'm doing good." Foster handed Tony a bottle of water and a few food items. He glanced around. This was the group Victoria usually traveled with. They were a mixture of drunks, drug addicts, and a few good people down on their luck, trying to figure things out. They watched out for each other. Tony tried to keep an eye out for those selling themselves for drugs and booze, and Victoria fell into that category.

Foster didn't know much about Tony, except other than smelling like a cheap bottle of wine most days, he seemed like the kind of man Foster might have liked in his past life.

"Have you seen Victoria lately?" Foster pointed to a spot where he noticed some of her things.

Tony dropped his gaze.

That was never good. It usually meant one of two things. The first one was that she was out pimping herself for drugs. Although, the last time he'd seen her, she looked like death. She was skin and bones, pale, but her skin had a yellowish tint. So did her eyes. She had these big black bags under them as well. He couldn't imagine anyone would give her money for sex, but then again, what did he know? He'd never lived that kind of life. While he'd seen her choose her addiction over their child, and he tried the drugs, he still struggled with how it all happened.

"When was the last time you saw her?" Foster asked.

"A couple of days ago, I think. I lose track of time," Tony admitted. "She didn't look right. Sick maybe. And she limped." He shrugged.

"If I give you some things, will you keep them for her?"

Tony lifted a blanket. "I have her valuables, so anything that won't go bad, I can save for her."

"Thanks. I'll come back in a few days." Foster pulled out his card with his cell number on it. "Find a way to reach me if she's in really bad shape, okay?"

"Sure thing." Tony organized the items that Foster dished out.

"You can keep some food and water for yourself."

"Thanks, man. Much appreciated." Tony nodded.

Foster spent the next hour wandering the streets, searching for Victoria, but with no luck. Instead of going home, he found himself at the new restaurant, the Blue Moon. It had been an old warehouse down the street from all the other food establishments. It had been an eyesore for years until three brothers bought the place and had Sutten and Tanner Construction renovate it.

He found an empty spot at the bar and ordered a bourbon.

"Hey, Foster."

Foster twisted his body. "Oh. Hi, Jared." He stretched out his arm. "How are you?"

"I'm doing well," Jared said. "Except for feeling like an old man." He glanced over his shoulder. "My wife thought it would be good to have dinner and drinks with our new neighbors down the street. They have a kid the same age as Bella, our youngest. Only, that's their oldest, and I feel like a dinosaur."

Foster laughed. He didn't know Jared all that well, but what he did know, he liked and respected.

Not to mention, Jared had been there the night Lisa, his precious daughter, had died.

"Age is just a number." Foster lifted his glass.

"Easy for you to say. Have you even hit forty yet?"

"Getting close," Foster admitted.

"Well, when you're fifty-seven, let's talk." Jared raked a hand across the top of his head. "Honestly, I wouldn't care, except my Bella is only fifteen and their son is the same age and it seems I'm the last to know they're boyfriend and girlfriend."

"Ryan knew?" Foster had gotten to know Jared's wife at a couple of local weddings. She was a lot of fun and most likely kept Jared on his toes. They had the kind of marriage that most people could only dream about. "And didn't tell you?"

"Bella didn't tell either one of us because she knew her mother would push her to bring it to me. But the hardest part is one of the Lake George Patrol troopers busted this kid and his friends doing shit they

9

shouldn't be doing last week. I haven't figured out how to deal with it yet."

"Drinking? Pot smoking? That kind of stuff?"

"If it were that, I'd be putting an end to it right now." Jared let out a long breath. "Especially at that age. I mean, I know kids will be kids. Trust me. I've got twin seventeen-year-old boys that some days I want to lock up and throw away the key. No, this was stupid horseplay on the lake, but someone could have gotten hurt. I can't have my daughter around that and I don't know how the parents are dealing with disciplining their teenager."

"That's a tough one, especially when some parents don't like to bring up their children's bad behavior with others."

"Worse when it's a state trooper." Jared arched a brow. "When Caitlyn was about the same age, she had one friend whose dad constantly tried to make their daughter out to be a perfect child until I had to bring them home in the back of my patrol car. It could have been worse, but I gave her the benefit of the doubt because I knew the family. After that, my kid wasn't allowed to hang out with his because I was power-hungry. I don't want this to turn into that, but shit, I'm not ready for my baby girl to have a boyfriend. It's bad enough Caitlyn has one. Hell, I'm struggling with the twins going off to college next year."

"Before you know it, you'll have a dozen grandkids."

"And I thought I liked you." Jared laughed, shaking his head. "I better get back to the table and address the elephant in the room."

"Good luck, man."

Jared waved his hand over his head as he made his way back to the patio outside.

Foster pulled out his cell and stared at Tonya's contact information. God, he was pathetic. Going down this road was a mistake.

Friends.

Shit.

Foster: *Everything okay with Tiki?*

Bubbles appeared immediately.

Tonya: *Calmed her down and sent her home. Did you watch the show?*

Foster: *I wouldn't dare do that without you. Went looking for Victoria. I'm a little worried about her. Haven't seen her in a while. Now I'm having a drink at the Blue Moon. They did a nice job with the bar. We'll have to come sometime.*

Crap. Why did he say that? It sounded like he was asking her on a date.

Tonya: *Maybe we can do a wedding planner meeting there.*

Phew. Glad she didn't go there, but now he was kind of insulted. This back and forth, flipping and flopping of both their emotions, was making him

11

crazy. They were friends and it was important to keep things on that level.

Foster: *Sounds like a plan. Sleep well. See you at your sister's wedding.*

No more bubbles.

He waved to the bartender. Time to get his check and head home. Tomorrow would be difficult. A year ago, he watched Tonya's other sister get married and it stirred something deep in his soul. These feelings he had for Tonya conflicted him. He enjoyed her company. Her kindness. She was the sweetest, most genuine person he'd ever met. Tomorrow, he'd watch her other sister marry the love of her life. He'd take them on a boat ride around the bay and he'd relish in the thought that he'd brought them a little piece of heaven.

His daughter, Lisa, would love that.

She was only seven when she passed, but she loved weddings. She would walk around the house in heels and a pillowcase, carrying anything that she could pretend were flowers. She would tell him that someday he was going to lose her to her knight in shining armor and he'd scoop her up in his arms and promise her that he'd find the finest boat and drive her and her prince around the lake.

If he couldn't do it for his precious baby, he'd do it for every other woman who had a daddy who loved them.

2

Tonya made her way from the crowd on the front lawn of her childhood home and headed toward the dock. The sun hung high in a bright-blue sky over the crystal-clear waters of Lake George.

Her happy place.

But today, there was a sense of melancholy she couldn't shake.

Always a bridesmaid, never a bride.

That thought had been playing in Tonya's mind for weeks leading up to her sister's wedding. She wasn't jealous of Tiki's happiness with Lake. Or the fact that she was the only Johnson sister left not married since Tayla got married a year ago.

She wanted her sisters to have all their dreams come true. She wanted to be part of every aspect of both her sisters' lives. They meant the world to her and she would do anything for them.

But that didn't mean she didn't want her knight in shining armor to lift her into his arms, drop her in his boat, and ride off into the sunset with her wedding veil flowing in the breeze. Okay, maybe not the veil at this point, but she knew what she wanted.

It was an image she'd conjured a million times ever since she'd fallen for Foster, but not once had she ever made her feelings known, at least not verbally. A few times she thought they had come through in other ways, but nothing ever happened.

"Hey, sweetheart," her grandfather called from a folding chair near the sundeck. His voice cracked, and he coughed. "Have you taken my advice?" He glanced over his shoulder and nodded toward Foster and his shiny wedding boat.

Foster had been acting strange all day. Well, odd for him. He attended the wedding but hung out in the background, standing off to the side, as if he wasn't supposed to be there. He'd been sent an invitation. He wasn't there only as *the wedding driver*. He was there as a close family friend.

Her friend.

This morning when she called, he went into all the reasons why, since she was in the wedding party, it didn't make sense for her to come over and bring the boat to the venue like she had with other clients.

She had a dozen retorts, but didn't use a single one.

"I thought about it last night, but I swear, he's not interested." She leaned over and kissed her grandpa's cheek. In the last year, it seemed he'd aged more than usual. His energy was down, and he wasn't doing all the things he loved the same way, and even though he never complained, Tonya worried about him. "Before you lecture me, it's not like I've never put myself out there or made subtle hints."

"I know you, Tonya. You've never expressed your wants and needs well." Her grandfather shook his head, rubbing his chin with his thumb and forefinger. "I remember when you were about seven, and I took you, and only you, to go see Santa. You let five little boys and girls go ahead of you."

"That's because they were either crying or their parents had little babies with them that were crying. Or one little girl had to pee so bad I thought she was going to do it right there in line. I was being kind."

"What about the fact that when you finally got to Santa, you told him that you didn't need anything."

She never liked suggesting gifts for herself. It felt pretentious to tell anyone what to buy as a present, yet she had no problem telling brides to make sure they told everyone where their registry was so that they got exactly what they wanted and not five of everything. But her grandpa wasn't really talking about that. It had more to do with the fact that she didn't like to be the center of attention. She always preferred to be behind the scenes of anything. She hated surprise parties. Hell, she never wanted to even have a regular birthday party. The few times she did have one, she would have anxiety issues when the kids would gather around her to open the gifts. When she turned twelve years old, she finally found her voice and told her parents to stop planning parties with her friends and keep it to her sisters and a family dinner.

Lucky for her, they respected that and to this day, they kept it simple. But finding her voice was half the battle. Expressing it was the rest—two things she didn't always do.

"I've never wanted for anything," she said.

"Except Foster."

"Not a good comparison, Grandpa," she said. "Things with him are complicated."

Foster could only be described as a lone wolf. He spent his time tinkering on his house and his cabin in the woods. When he wasn't doing that, he was checking on his ex-wife, who was currently homeless, something Foster wanted to change, but Victoria wouldn't even go to a shelter, much less consider living in Foster's cabin or boathouse, unless she was sober, which hadn't happened in three years.

Outside of that, Foster had his wedding business and then did side work for Sutten and Tanner Construction, a local company. Lately, he'd been working longer hours for Doug and Jim and enjoying it. That made Tonya happy. It seemed like Foster was finding his groove. He needed that so he could live in the present, not the past all the time.

"Perhaps." He waggled his finger. "But you've never told him that you have feelings for him. All you've ever done is half-assed it because you're afraid. Just like with Santa. Or with a lot of things because you don't like to rock the boat."

"What is that supposed to mean?" She shifted her gaze to the dock, where Foster waited for the bride and groom. He'd been unusually nervous, which was never like him on wedding days. He loved nuptials. He was an old sap when it came to romance. It might not be for him, but he appreciated the ritual for others.

Tiki's wedding had been bigger and required more planning than Tayla's intimate ceremony. Tiki had been impressed with Tonya's negotiating abilities. She had even teased Tonya about how *ruthless* she'd been in getting the best price for the centerpieces for the table. That had made Tonya laugh. She wouldn't have described herself that way at all. It was her job to help the bride and groom have the most special day within their budget. All she did was talk the vendor into a price she knew he could handle and still turn a profit.

She understood where Tiki was coming from because it wasn't like Tonya to be outspoken in general.

"The entire reason you never told Santa what you really wanted was out of fear. You didn't want to be disappointed on Christmas morning. You've always believed it's better to not have high expectations."

That was a true statement and one she wasn't going to argue. Her grandfather had roundabout ways of getting to his point. The analogies didn't always make sense, but his intentions did, and right now, he'd nailed it. When it came to Foster, she didn't think it was a good idea to push. It had less to do with not wanting to be hurt if he rejected her feelings, but his friendship was more important and she wanted to make sure he'd always be in her life.

"I understand you're scared," her grandfather said. "What's the worst thing that can happen if you put your heart on the line?"

Of all the people in the world, she could be the most honest with her grandfather, especially now that both her sisters had gotten married. It wasn't that she couldn't bare her soul to Tiki and Tayla, because she absolutely could. It was that she didn't want to constantly hear their positive interjections about how love would happen for her when it was her time. That some awesome man was wandering the area, looking for the perfect woman, and it was time to play the field. One of her sisters—she couldn't remember which one—had even suggested that might make Foster think about making a move.

Ugh. That felt like manipulation.

"That I make things awkward and could change our friendship and our working relationship. I don't want to risk losing him forever. He's a good friend. I want to keep it that way."

"I doubt that you will make it weird by putting your feelings out there. I have faith you won't do that. Neither will he. But you'll never know if you sit there and keep your emotions bottled up inside."

This had been her grandpa's mantra for the last couple of years. Lately, however, he'd been pushing harder than usual, bringing it up almost every time he saw her, and she started to wonder if maybe he was right. What made it all worse was the last few times she'd been with Foster, like last night, he'd been giving her signals.

Of course, she could be misreading those simply because she was madly in love with the man.

"You know it's not that simple, especially now." She had a million excuses as to why she shouldn't express her feelings. It was never the right time. Or something in one of their lives got complicated. But the bottom line was she was terrified so she avoided it.

"Why? Because Victoria is living on the streets and using? She's been doing that on and off since he divorced her. That is nothing new."

"She went missing for an entire month this past winter. It was terrifying for Foster. He feels responsible for her for some reason. She's spiraling out of control and he's concerned. She hasn't stopped using for three years. That's the longest she's been on a binge and—"

"I'm well aware of how Foster worries about his ex-wife. When he and I have gone into the village, he's always looked for her to give her food and check on her. When he can't find her, he does tend to panic," her grandfather said. "But Foster can't save his ex-wife, and while he tries to protect her, deep down he knows her safety is out of his hands because he walks away even when he can't find her. Slowly, he's been distancing himself from her; even if you don't see it, or he doesn't accept it, that's the reality."

Tonya had been with Foster when he'd searched the streets looking for Victoria and came up empty-handed. The first time he never stressed. But if it lasted a week or more, that's when the panic set in and he'd spend every waking moment checking known crack houses and all her old stomping grounds. The problem with Foster when it came to his ex-wife was he felt as though he let her and their daughter down. He still carried tremendous guilt over Lisa's death and what he believed was his role.

Her grandfather took her hand. "There is room for you in his heart, but you have to tell him how you feel and give him a chance to open up to you. He's been alone for a long time and he holds his grief close to his soul. I can understand why he does that." Her grandpa tapped his chest. "Foster is only torturing himself because he holds himself responsible for what happened."

Foster's loss cut deep. It was palpable and there was nothing anyone could do to help him move past it.

"The death of a child isn't something you get over," she said. "You know that better than anyone."

"That's not what I'm saying at all." Her grandpa squeezed her hand. "You love him and you're going to be stuck right here in this moment in life if you don't either walk away from your feelings or put them all on the line so you have the opportunity to either be with him or move on. The same goes for him. The thing with his emotions is, he's closed himself off to the point his circle is so small that we're the only ones he has let into his life in years. I believe he cares for you, but he's not going to be the one to take the first step. You have to do it."

She knew her grandfather was right. She had been standing still for years and it was time to do something about it. She felt that last night.

Leaning in, she kissed her granddad's cheek. "I'm going to finally listen to you and take your advice."

"That's my girl."

She squared her shoulders and headed down to the dock where Foster waited for Tiki and Lake. Her heart hammered in her chest, as it often did when she approached the man she'd been in love with for as long as she could remember.

"Hey," she managed to croak out. "Need a hand?"

"Do you think your sister will be much longer?" Foster asked, barely glancing in her direction as he fiddled with a few things on his old-fashioned wooden boat. It was strange that he'd avoided her so adamantly on this day, but she wasn't going to let him any longer.

"I'm sure she'll be down in a few minutes." Tonya leaned against the post and stared at a sailboat floating in the center of the bay. The tall mast reached for the clear blue sky. The lines smacked against the metal as the boat rocked from the waves created by the boats buzzing around the bay.

"Knowing your mother, she's making her say goodbye to each guest personally." Foster smiled.

"That sounds about right," Tonya said. "So, what's the plan? Around Harris and Sandy Bay? Or are you going to go around Long Island?"

"We went over the boat ride when we sat down and talked about it this morning."

"You're dropping them at their house, right?"

Foster hopped onto the dock and adjusted his hat. "That's the plan, but you knew that." He arched a brow. "What's going on with you?" He inched closer, reaching out, circling his strong fingers around her forearm.

The moment his skin touched hers, an electric shock pulsed through her system.

Staring into the depths of his tender blue eyes, she cleared her throat and searched her mind for the right words. The perfect words.

"Why don't you see me?" Inwardly, she groaned. That wasn't what she wanted to say. Not even close. She wasn't even sure that made any sense.

He tilted his head. "Of course I see you. You're standing right in front of me."

"That's not what I meant."

Slowly, he blinked. His hand ran up and down her arm. "I know," he whispered. "I'm not blind. And I'm not stupid. Insensitive at times, but not unaware that somewhere things shifted." He took in a deep breath and let it out slowly.

"Shifted. That's what you're calling my feelings?"

He lifted his hat and raked a hand through his thick, dark hair. "We've known each other a long time. You were the first wedding planner to give me business when everyone else thought my idea was nutty."

"It's not the best business model when the majority of our weather is freezing cold, but it's a sweet idea and I thought it was a creative way for people to celebrate."

"I appreciate that." He smiled. "Through the years, you've been a good friend to me—so has your family—and I value that. I wouldn't want to lose it by mucking up the waters."

"You sound like what I've been telling myself for a long time."

"But now you've voiced it." He placed his hat back on his head and took a step back, turning toward the lake. "We can't put it back in a bottle and pretend it's not there like we've been doing."

"I'm not sure what you mean by that." Her pulse beat in the center of her throat. She couldn't swallow. She glanced over her shoulder, grateful that her sister and Lake had yet to even make it to the pathway.

He stuffed his hands in his pockets. "I've always seen you, but you have made it very easy for me to keep you at arm's length because you give me space. You've never made your feelings known through words, or even actions. I know they exist. I can feel them; however, you don't express them, allowing me the freedom to continue to do what I've done since Lisa died, and that's pretty much exist on being numb."

"What are you saying?" She clutched her chest.

It was rare that Foster ever discussed his daughter. He was a private man who kept his personal torment to himself. Occasionally, when his ex-wife would go missing, he'd open up about his past, but he never let her in too deep.

He turned, catching her gaze with more intensity than she was used to coming from him. "I've always been afraid you might tell me how you feel. Last night, when I asked you to stay, I figured it was a mistake. I worried I might even cross the line. I've never been sure what I'd do if either of us ever made a move. I'm still not sure."

"We're talking in circles." She rubbed her temple.

"I'm sorry. I didn't mean to do that," he said. "Tell me what you want."

She admired his bluntness and now it was her turn to do the same. "How about a boat ride?"

"I've given you plenty." He chuckled. "You almost always help me put her away after I take your clients for a ride. Not to mention other times when helping your family with different things."

She reached for a hair tie to put her locks into a ponytail, but there was none around her wrist. Shit. Her mother had made her remove it for the wedding. She always carried one in case she needed to fiddle to calm her nerves. Five times today she'd wanted to put her hair up and each time she ended up wiggling her fingers and darting her gaze while having an uncomfortable conversation with someone.

Only this time, she wasn't going to hide her feelings. "I was thinking more along the lines of heading up to West Dollar Island with a picnic or something."

"I see." He rubbed his chin with his thumb and forefinger. "You're talking about going on a date."

Her heart thumped to her throat and then dropped into her stomach like a brick. "That's what I'm asking." The chatter of wedding guests clapping and cheering grew louder. She stole a quick glance toward the front lawn. Tiki and Lake were making their way down toward the docks, hugging and waving to family and friends.

Tonya had minutes to firm this up.

"All right. Do you have plans tomorrow?" He inched closer. Too close. So close the tips of his toes touched hers.

"I don't."

"You do now." He lifted his hat and pressed his lips on her cheek, letting them linger. They stayed there for a good minute. And then another one. It wasn't awkward, but it wasn't a simple kiss on the cheek, either. "Be at my place by nine."

"Okay," she managed to croak out.

"Bring a bathing suit, sunscreen, and towel. I'll take care of everything else." He stepped onto the boat and pointed. "Here comes the bride and groom."

Glancing over her shoulder, she swallowed the thick thump that had formed in her throat. This was exactly what she'd wanted when she decided to follow her heart and tell Foster she wanted to explore more than a friendship. Only, she expected to be shot down. She had mentally prepared herself for him to tell her it was best if they didn't step out of the zone they were in, not jump off the cliff.

Tiki glided onto the dock in her fabulous wedding dress designed by their sister. Lake was all smiles as he turned and waved to the crowd.

"Thanks. This was the best party ever." Tiki

handed Tonya her bouquet before pulling her in for a brief hug. "You're amazing."

"Right back at you, sis." Tonya smiled. "Have a great honeymoon." She turned her attention to the groom. "You better treat my sister like a queen."

"You know I will." Lake gave her a big hug. "We'll see you in a week." He took his bride's hand and helped her onto Foster's boat.

Tonya undid both the bow and stern lines with happy tears shining in her eyes.

"See you tomorrow." Foster tipped his hat and tapped the throttle.

Tiki tilted her head and narrowed her stare, but said nothing as the boat picked up speed, heading out into the bay.

Tonya blew out a long breath.

Time to go bathing suit shopping in Tayla's new collection.

3

*F*oster hadn't been on a date since he married at twenty-two years old, fifteen years ago. His marriage had lasted eight years, and only the first couple could have been considered good, although that was debatable. His daughter was the only reason he could even describe that time in his life as decent.

However, there was nothing left to try to salvage by the time Lisa had turned three. Victoria had totally checked out of life. Things went from bad to worse, and then Lisa died.

He blamed himself. He knew he shouldn't, but he couldn't help it.

"Here you go." Foster set a vodka tonic in front of Doug Tanner and sat on the sundeck in the Adirondack chair that overlooked Warner Bay. He bought this property six months after Lisa had passed. He had no desire to rebuild the family home he'd shared with Victoria, so he sold it to Doug and his partner, who turned it into an amazing home and flipped it for a pretty penny.

That had surprised Foster, considering the stigma of the fire that had burned the original home to the ground, killing his daughter.

"Cheers." Doug tapped the plastic glass. "So, am I here because you're finally going to let me and my father-in-law have at this place and totally renovate it for you?"

Foster laughed. "I like tinkering with it, and I know you and Jim. You'll want to come in like a wrecking ball."

"What is your reluctance in doing the work within a six-month timeframe? This property is amazing. The location is perfection. You've got a killer view. I know you don't want some massive, overstated home. But you could do something spectacular with a rustic feel. And that cabin could be updated and rented more often."

If nothing else, Foster could be honest with himself. He'd been doing that soul-searching for years. He continued with therapy, seeing a counselor twice a month to deal with his grief.

And his guilt.

Along with all the reasons he didn't want to move forward with his life.

That included making a real home for himself and what that might mean if he did.

However, he never voiced any of those reasons to anyone other than his therapist. That would make it real. That would mean he had to take both feet out of the past and move them into the present. It was hard enough dealing with his emotions when it came to Tonya.

Everything changed when he decided to take Tonya on a date. It wasn't like he hadn't thought about it. He had. Day and night. For weeks. Months.

Hell, for the last couple of years, she'd haunted his dreams. She filled his daily thoughts. No matter what he did, he couldn't shake how she'd gotten under his skin, but as long as she didn't pursue him, he could pretend she didn't care.

That he had no feelings at all. It was easy for him to bury them. Like he did with his past. Only, Tonya had touched his soul and opened his heart.

"Truth?" Foster asked.

"Only if you want to give it to me." Doug was easy to hang out with because he didn't pressure Foster into opening up and sharing.

Foster took a long, slow sip of his drink. "My ex-wife has been on a downward spiral for a long time. When I saw her last, she didn't look good. The whites of her eyes were yellow. If she weighed a hundred pounds, I'd be shocked. I tried to get her to go to the hospital, but she told me she'd leave. Refuse treatment. Or tell them I kidnapped her. It's like she's slowly killing herself."

"I know how hard living on the streets can be. I can't imagine doing it while battling addiction. I know my biological parents suffered, but I don't remember it," Doug said softly. He had shared his life story with Foster when they first met and while his teenage years were heartbreaking, he had been given a chance at life when Jim Sutten welcomed him into his home and taught him a trade.

Doug took the opportunity he'd been given. He did everything Jim asked him to do. He'd been a scared fifteen-year-old boy with nowhere to go and the smarts to understand if he didn't grab ahold of the lifeline he'd been given, he'd probably be dead by now.

"Victoria has totally given up at this point," Foster admitted. "Her parents would rather I stop looking for her and giving her food. They believe I'm enabling her. They think that I'm exacerbating the problem. To them, she died the same day Lisa did."

"It's a fine line that you're walking with Victoria. Believe me, I know. There is only so much you can do."

Foster had no idea if what he did for Victoria was for her own good or to appease some of his own guilt for the years of anger and resentment.

Which he still harbored because at the end of the

day, it was due to Victoria's drug abuse that their home burned down and their daughter had died.

"If I finish this house, I'm officially starting over. I'm not sure I'm ready," Foster said. "Or that I can. My existence seems lonely and sad, but I'm not unhappy."

"That's a pretty telling statement." Doug shifted in his chair. He leaned forward, resting his elbows on his knees. "When Jim first took me in, I didn't believe I deserved his kindness. I was always waiting for it to end. Waiting for him to tell me to leave. He had a young daughter to think about and I could have been a bad decision. For the first year or two, I would wake up every morning and think this was going to be the day that Jim changed his mind. But he never did."

"Did you ever ask him why he took the risk of bringing a homeless kid into his house as a single father?"

Doug nodded. "It's odd to be nine years older than your wife and nine years younger than your father-in-law. But when I came into their lives, Jim was focused on getting his business off the ground and being the best father to Stacey. She was quite the precarious little girl. Outgoing and outspoken even at six. Jim barely dated. He didn't socialize. He brought me in, taught me his trade, put me through school, and we became best friends and eventually partners. When my first wife was murdered about the time my feelings for Stacey shifted from friends to something more, Jim and I sat down and talked about why he took me in. He didn't understand it at the time, but if you believe in fate, as he does these days, it was as if I was sent there to be first his friend and then Stacey's husband. All the while, giving me a chance at life."

"That's quite the profound statement."

"It is. And I believe, after everything Stacey and I went through, that while life since then has been calm, we have no idea what it could throw at us. Now that I have kids of my own, a wife who keeps saying she's going to retire her badge, but never does, and a father-in-law as a business partner and a best friend, taking all those risks was worth it because if we hadn't, we'd all probably live a life full of regrets."

"Part of my problem is I took that risk the day I married Victoria."

"Did you love her?" Doug asked. "Because I didn't love my first wife. I thought I knew what love was, or what I wanted it to look like, but it wasn't that."

"She was pregnant. With my baby."

"So was Mary. But she miscarried. And then everything went to shit."

A day didn't go by where Foster didn't conjure up happy memories of his daughter. Lisa loved life. She was a happy kid, despite Victoria's addiction. Foster knew he would have ended up divorced even if the fire had never happened. He stayed with Victoria for as long as he did for the sake of his child.

In hindsight, he realized that was a mistake.

He carried that guilt in his heart. It cut deep into his soul.

"What is it that you're honestly afraid of?" Doug asked.

"That's a long list, man," Foster said. "I know I need to make some changes and I did something that pushes me into living life again, but I worry it might be a huge mistake." Foster kept his focus on a sailboat tacking across the bay in the slight westerly breeze.

"That's cryptic."

Foster chuckled. "This is uncomfortable for me to talk about. I've spent the last seven years trying to keep my life as private as possible. I've avoided relationships and friendships, but in the last couple of years, I've developed deeper connections."

"I hope you consider me a close friend."

"I do. The best. You and Jim have been very good to me." Foster nodded. "It's just that when it comes to women, I don't know how to do anything other than small talk and tomorrow I'm going on a date. I'm totally out of my element."

"Tonya?"

"How'd you know I was taking her out?"

"You and she are about as obvious as Stacey and I were." Doug laughed. "Everyone can see that there's something between the two of you. Even if you don't."

Foster took a gulp of his beverage. It wasn't so

much that he cared if people knew. Or thought the two of them should be a couple. The problem was, he wasn't sure he could do more than prove to himself this wasn't a good idea. Or maybe there wasn't a love connection because he couldn't be all in. He still had this weird sense of obligation to his ex-wife he couldn't shake.

"I can see it bothers you that I—and others—have noticed you have an affection for Tonya."

"I guess it does a little. I thought I was being private about my feelings. She wasn't totally shocked, but she was thrown for a loop that I wanted to go out with her. What I'm struggling with right now is twofold. I'm worried I'm going to end up hurting Tonya because I'm a broken man. And I have no idea how to handle myself on a date other than we're going on a picnic."

"You're not as broken as you think you are," Doug said. "Going on this date is a step in the right direction, so let's focus on that. Are you going on the lake?"

"Yeah," Foster said. "I'm packing fried chicken and all the fixings. I thought we'd go cliff jumping too. But I have no idea what to talk about or how to act. I seriously haven't taken out a woman since my daughter died. I'm not kidding."

"Wow." Doug stared at him with wide eyes. "Okay. What do you and Tonya normally talk about?"

"Her clients. Wedding stuff. This house and what

I should do with it. Tayla and her boutique and clothing lines. Tiki and her publishing career. Occasionally we get into Victoria and all of that, but I honestly try to avoid the conversation. However, Tonya does most of the chatting. But it all feels so strange now. The pressure that's sitting on the center of my chest is making it hard to breathe. I feel like I need to be the one in the driver's seat and I don't like that sensation."

"When Stacey and I first got together, things were intense. It shifted so quickly that it felt like I got hit by a train."

"I can't say the same." Foster glanced toward the sky, noting the position of the Big Dipper. "I've been hyperaware of her for a long time and I know she's had feelings for me. But because of my situation and the way I am, she's always given me space. And I've taken it. I've been secretly hoping some man will come and sweep her off her feet, but at the same time, I get jealous of the idea."

"What changed and set this date in motion?"

"Her sister's wedding, for one, and why should she sit around and wait for me to make a move? I was never going to do it."

"No offense, man, but that just kind of makes you an asshole," Doug said. "Especially considering the fact that you do care about her."

Foster didn't entirely agree with that statement. "When my daughter died, I wasn't sure I could ever have any kind of life again. I'm honestly still not sure I can, which is another reason I'm concerned about this date."

"Have you told Tonya that?"

"No," Foster admitted.

"That's a topic to discuss."

"That's not very date like."

"Maybe not," Doug said. "But if there's going to be a second, it puts her in a position to go into this with her eyes wide open."

"But I'm also worried about my emotions over my past. I was so angry at my ex-wife for doing drugs in the house. I was filled with hatred for myself for even leaving Lisa alone with her mother. I knew I couldn't trust her, yet I went out anyway. I still carry enormous guilt with me and it often eats at my ability to have deep interpersonal relationships. It's why I've never dated and certainly why I haven't asked Tonya out. She's a special girl and she deserves the best."

"I can't imagine what you've been through," Doug said. "Those had to have been some dark days."

At least Doug didn't try to tell Foster that it wasn't his fault and that time would heal his wounds.

Neither was true.

"It has taken a lot of therapy to get me to this place and while I wouldn't call myself happy, I'm not unhappy."

"You exist."

"That's a good way to put it." Foster shifted his

gaze and sipped his drink. It felt good to talk with a friend about the things he saved for his therapist, who told him he needed to get out there and do some male bonding anyway.

This was a good start. He had thought about calling Gael, but he was married to Tonya's sister and that might be mixing too much family. Besides, he thought Doug might understand his situation the best.

"I'll be honest." Doug leaned forward. "I can't even wrap my brain around what you've gone through. When I try, tears fill my eyes, my heart hurts more than I've ever experienced in my entire life, and I have to stop. I want to go hug and kiss my kids until they tell me I'm suffocating them."

"I think that's normal for any parent."

Doug tapped his chest. "Maybe, and I won't pretend to have any idea of what I would do in your shoes because I can't even walk in them. However, we both know there are others who do know what it's like to be you. I'm no expert in grief. That said, I do know about loneliness and building walls to keep others out. That's no way to live. I believe you owe it to yourself, and your daughter, to give this life a chance. To open your heart to Tonya and to be honest with her about what you're thinking and feeling. Existing doesn't do Lisa's memory any favors and it's only slowly killing your soul."

That wasn't the first time Foster had heard that. Victoria's parents had been hammering that into his brain for years. So had his therapist, though she'd been nicer about it.

And then there was Foster's mother. She desperately wanted him to climb out of his hermit shell.

"Okay. For argument's sake, let's say that tomorrow goes well and a second date happens. How did you go from being best friends with Stacey, to being her boyfriend during a time when you were under investigation for murder?"

"I jumped in with two feet and prayed her father didn't kill me."

Foster laughed. "You've got to have better advice for me than that."

"It's the honest truth," Doug said. "Don't overthink it, like you're doing right now. Put one foot in front of the other and be yourself. She's already invested, so she's yours to lose."

Foster let out a long breath. "That just made it worse."

"You're going to be fine. Tell her what's going on in your mind and get yourself out of your head." Doug glanced at his watch. "I better get going. The kids might be getting older, but bedtime is one of those things that can turn into a madhouse. The youngest wants to do what my twelve-year-old is doing, and my daughter is a little drama queen sometimes."

"Thanks for stopping by. I appreciate the chat."

"Anytime. You still plan on helping out on the Mason project next week, right?" Doug stood.

"Absolutely."

Doug gave his shoulder a good squeeze before heading toward the path that led to the driveway.

Foster took out his cell and pulled up his favorites.

He had two.

His mother.

And Tonya.

That spoke volumes.

He tapped Tonya's picture. He wasn't sure why or what he was going to say.

She picked up on the third ring. "Hello?"

"Hey. It's Foster."

"I know," she said. "Is everything okay?"

Half the time he called her it was about business. The other half, it was about his ex-wife and him needing help. It was never to have a conversation about her or what she was thinking and feeling.

It was about time that changed.

"Yeah. I was just sitting outside, enjoying a drink, watching the stars, and I thought of you."

"Huh?"

He chuckled. That had to have sounded weird, but oddly, it didn't feel strange rolling off his tongue. "I wanted to make sure you liked the cold fried chicken and all the trimmings from the deli down the street from my house."

"I love it," she said. "But you knew that."

That was true. He did. "Shall I pack red or white wine?"

"Either is fine with me."

He could tell he'd caught her off guard. He wasn't sure if that was a good thing or a bad thing. One thing he knew for sure was that she loved chocolate. He always had little chocolate treats on his boat and she'd laugh and steal an entire handful every time she'd disembark.

Earlier, at her sister's wedding, he watched her eat two pieces of chocolate cake. He'd make sure he had a decadent dessert to share after lunch.

"I'll bring a bottle of both and we can decide what we're feeling when we get there." This was definitely good practice for small talk, but he knew he needed to dig deeper. He cared about Tonya as a friend and no matter what happened, he didn't want to hurt her and she needed to understand that. He just wasn't sure how to go from the light stuff to what his heart was afraid of. "How'd the cleanup go of your parents' place? I told them I could have come over." That wasn't the transition he was looking for, but over the phone wasn't the right time.

"Gael hired a crew to do everything. I'm already home."

"Did you get your new sofa?" Tonya had moved into Jared and Ryan Blake's carriage house on Cleverdale, not far from her parents' house. It was a nice one-bedroom rental that Jared cut her a big break on while she saved her money so she could buy a place on the lake.

"Not yet. It's back-ordered for another month."

"That sucks. I know how much you've been looking forward to that."

"I don't know. I'm thinking about canceling it."

"Why?" he asked.

"It was more than I wanted to spend."

He had no idea what her financial situation was other than it was night and day from his. He'd been born into money. Then he married it. However, Victoria's parents cut her off when they found out she was using after Lisa had been born.

When he met his ex-wife and him got serious, she'd been clean and sober. He valued that and chose not to drink. It had been an easy decision. As a matter of fact, he didn't have a drop of alcohol until after his daughter had died. He'd seen firsthand what addiction could do to a person—to a family—and he never wanted to put his mother through what Victoria put him or her parents through.

He never questioned Victoria's parents' decision to take away their daughter's ability to withdraw money from the family bank accounts. It didn't matter. He had more than enough and in his previous career in sales, he certainly made a pretty penny. He also made sure that his wife didn't have access to large sums, but that didn't stop her from selling her designer purses or her daughter's toys.

But money didn't make anyone happy.

"It's a quality sofa. It will last a long time. Keep it," he said. "Sometimes you need to splurge on yourself."

"That's what Ryan said."

"Ryan's a smart woman." Foster stood. He collected his glass and headed toward the main house. "It's getting late and I should let you get some sleep. I'll see you in the morning."

"Good night, Foster."

"Sweet dreams." He ended the call, tucking the cell in his back pocket. For the first time in a long time, the blood in Foster's veins ran hot.

4

"Thanks for coming over." Tonya handed a cup of coffee to her sister before easing herself down into one of the Adirondack chairs on the side yard that Jared and his wife allowed her to use. It hadn't been easy for her to call her sister. Part of her had thought about chatting with Ryan. Their love story had been more similar because Ryan had known Jared her entire life. They had been friends long before they had ever started dating. Jared had also lost a child and understood Foster's pain.

However, Ryan took their youngest child to an event and wouldn't return for a few hours. It was probably for the best. Foster had always been a private man and his history with his ex-wife had played out in a very public way. The fire and the death of Lisa had been front-page news, but Foster did his best to remain out of the public eye. He didn't comment when the reporters stuck microphones in his face. He didn't once do an interview.

The only thing he did was appear in court to beg the judge for leniency when sentencing his wife for the involuntary manslaughter of their child and to ask that Victoria receive treatment for her addiction. Not many men would do that. The judge heard Foster, and Victoria spent a year in jail and two years on probation.

But her rehab didn't stick.

"I know you're busy with the new line and the boutique sale this weekend," Tonya said. "So it means a lot to me that you'd drop everything to spend a half hour with your little sister."

"Gael headed over early this morning," Tayla said. "He and my assistant can handle opening the shop, no problem."

"I'm a little surprised by how good he is with a sewing machine."

"He's not that good." Tayla laughed. "I only allow him to do hems. And only under the strictest of supervision, but he's to be commended for his dedication. Not to mention, he's the best husband ever."

Gael had been by Tayla's side through a lot of shit. He'd helped her see how she'd put her career before everything and how it was slowly destroying her sense of self.

Not to mention her relationships with her family, especially her sisters. When Tayla had moved to New

York City, she had promised Tiki and Tonya that she would always be there for them, but slowly, that changed.

Tayla changed. She became selfish and was so wrapped up in her career and becoming the best designer the fashion world had ever seen, she stopped being a sister.

Until she came home for a family reunion and met Gael. He showed her what was at stake.

Of course, Gael had lost so much. He'd been hyper-focused on his job and being at the top of the game. In doing so, he'd forgotten what was truly important, and by the time he did, he'd lost everyone he held dear.

"He is one of the good guys." Tonya blew into her mug before taking a slow sip. She stared out at the boats humming up and down the shoreline. It was a beautiful start to a Sunday morning. She had only a half hour left before hopping in her car and heading over to Foster's place.

She'd wanted this for so long but never thought it possible. Her sisters had told her to go for it, but she always came up with reasons to give Foster his space.

It was either Victoria was missing.

Or Victoria was using.

Or Victoria was in the hospital and drying out. There was hope she might get clean again and Foster needed her to be supportive, not trying to get in his pants.

Foster needed her friendship more than she needed a different kind of relationship. Eventually her sisters gave up pushing her, only nudging her every so often.

This last year, they went out of their way to comment about random men and how sexy they were and suggest that Tonya ask anyone out, but she never did. She was too hung up on Foster.

Now that she was about to go on an actual date with the man of her dreams, she wasn't sure how to proceed. It wasn't like she hadn't gone out with a man in the last few years. She'd had a few boyfriends. Foster had even met a couple of them. The whole point had been to get Foster out of her head.

And her heart.

But she ended up comparing everyone to Foster. Were they as kind and considerate to those around them? Did they tip as generously as he did? Were they as compassionate about other people and what they might be going through in their lives? If any man she went out with didn't measure up to the man she knew Foster to be, that was it, the relationship was over. That certainly didn't help her move beyond her feelings for Foster. If anything, it kept her in this never-ending cycle.

"Thank you for letting me steal a bathing suit that hasn't hit the market yet," Tonya said.

"Anything for you. Besides, you're a walking

advertisement for me," Tayla said. "But that's not why I'm here, so let's get to the heart of the matter."

"I'm so nervous. Foster called me last night. For no reason. He's never done that before. At first I thought he was going to cancel, but then he started asking me questions about our plans. It was weird."

"Did you ever think maybe he's feeling all the same things that you are?"

"I struggle with that concept. I mean, he says he's thought about it, and maybe he has. But I've daydreamed about this for years and now that it's happening, I'm freaking out." Tonya had tossed and turned all night. Every time she closed her eyes, Foster was there, taunting her with his wickedly subtle smile. When she opened them, her mind went over every possible scenario of today's events. The things that could go right.

And the things that could go wrong.

Sadly, she focused on the latter.

"You and Foster have a lot of history. It's going to be both easy and hard to slide into a romantic relationship."

"And you know this how?" Tonya lowered her chin and stared at her sister with a smirk.

Since college, Tayla spent her time building her career. She lost herself in it and had no time for boyfriends.

"I've had friends that I've hopped into bed with," Tayla said with a narrowed expression. "The dinner part is easy because you're comfortable with each other. But the getting naked part can be awkward. And in your case, you put Foster on a pedestal. He might not live up to your high expectations."

"You're not helping and that's not what I wanted to discuss anyway."

"Right." Tayla laughed. "Listen. The problem here is that you've put the cart before the horse. You're already in love with him."

"I shouldn't have called you over." Tonya loved her sister more than anything. Over the last year, her bluntness had settled into more of a *rough around the edges* truth, but she still always spoke her opinions when asked. That sometimes could be a hard pill to swallow. Like right now. However, if Tonya was being honest with herself, it was necessary to accept the fact that she did love Foster. She just wasn't willing to admit it to anyone else, not even her sisters.

"You're overthinking all of this. Go into it like every other time you see him. Don't think of this as something different. It's just another lunch meeting about work, yet you're talking about everything but. Make sense?"

"No. Things have changed and I'm scared. You know one of Grandpa's old sayings—*be careful what you ask for*—well, that's what I woke up to. I've wanted this for the last three years. Maybe longer. What if he kisses me and I hate it? Or worse, he doesn't like it. What if the date is so horrible that we can't ever be around each other again? My mind is going a mile a minute and I can't settle it down no matter how hard I try, and trust me, I've been doing every trick in the book to try to relax. I was even considering taking a gummy, now that it's legal. But then I don't want to be acting all weird and mushy like the last time I took one."

Tayla shook her head. "Yeah. We don't want that." She set her mug down on the small table, then took Tonya's hands and squeezed. "I might not have had any long-lasting relationships until Gael, but I know a little something about attitude." Tayla lowered her chin and arched a brow.

That brought a smile to Tonya's face. Her sister oozed confidence, even when Tonya and Tiki knew on the inside she was shaking like a leaf.

"If I let designers know I was worried about what they thought of me and my creations all the time, I wouldn't have gotten as far as I did. I know this isn't the same, but no matter what happens between you and Foster, you'll finally be able to get out of this place of limbo." Tayla squeezed. "This is a good thing. Either it will work out, or it won't."

Tonya inhaled sharply through her nose. The fresh summer air filled her nostrils. It smelled of sunshine and crisp morning dew.

Shit or get off the pot.

All her grandfather's words of wisdom were

flowing through her brain. They were all cliché, but there was a ring of truth to every single one.

She knew it was time.

The fact she finally told Foster she had feelings for him and that they were going on a date was the best thing that could have happened.

At least that's what she told herself.

"You want to know what's weird about all of this," Tonya said. "I feel like I've been walking around in a fog for so long and now that it's lifting, and I can see that I've been in a daze, I feel kind of stupid that I've waited so long or that I'm even so afraid. He's just a man. It's just a date. It shouldn't matter so much."

"It matters because you love him and that means there's something at stake." Tayla pursed her lips. "I wish you could bottle those feelings and set them aside so you could simply enjoy dating and getting to know Foster on a different level."

"That ship has sailed. But that brings me to why I asked you here this morning because I feel like this date will either be the door to more, or the end of it all."

"That's not true."

"Maybe not. But that's how I feel," Tonya said. "Generally, whenever Foster and I spend time together, we discuss weddings, and I often dominate the conversation. I talk about you and Gael or Grandpa and what's going on with him. Or Tiki and Lake and publishing.

Only very rarely does he ever select the topics. How do I get him talking about himself or have him direct the conversation without asking him a bunch of questions?"

"You could try silence."

"That only leads to me chatting away about random things or sitting around staring at nothing until one of us says good night."

"Bring up the last movie you watched that you think he might be interested in. Or television show you binged together. Or a book you read that you know he has. Anything that could get the two of you discussing something other than the usual suspects."

Tonya really didn't need her sister to tell her that, but it was the courage she wanted to hear. She glanced at her cell. "Shit. I need to get going." She jumped to her feet. "Thanks for coming over."

"Anytime. I'm always here for you if you want to talk." Tayla stood, pulling her sister in for a big bear hug. "I really want things to work out for you and Foster. I know I sometimes don't act like I do when I tell you to go find someone else, but now that you've got the ball rolling, I hope he can get past all his shit. He's been through a ton and you've given him lots of time and space to heal. But he can't keep hiding from life, and that's exactly what he's doing while you've stood still in yours. It's time."

Tonya nodded.

"Call me later?"

"I will." As Tonya made her way toward her car, her pulse kicked up a notch. Butterflies filled her gut.

She had a date.

With Foster.

Her life was going to change no matter how things turned out.

———

The ride up the lake was quiet. The morning sun shone bright in a cloud-free sky. There wasn't any breeze rolling off the mountains, but a fair amount of chop formed from all the boats.

Foster chalked up the silence to the immediate awkwardness between him and Tonya the moment she showed up at his place and they stood at the doorway staring at each other. He knew it would be like that, and he did his best to ease the weirdness by getting right in the boat and heading north.

However, now that they were in front of the picnic island, his heart pounded like a hammer. "I can't believe how busy it is up here today." There wasn't even a free dock, and four other boats were waiting to park.

"It's a beautiful day," Tonya said. "I'm not surprised it's this busy considering last weekend was so chilly."

"How about we go see if there's a room over in Paradise Bay, and we can just hang out there?"

"Sounds like a plan." She smiled, adjusting her sunglasses.

He maneuvered the boat around the others waiting and headed toward the east side of the lake. Once he was up to speed, he boldly lifted his arm and rested it over the back of the seat. He wanted her to know that he did acknowledge that this was indeed different from any other time they spent together. Yesterday, they declared today would be a date, yet it hadn't felt that way. He ran his finger across her bare shoulder. That should help move things along.

As soon as he approached the mouth of the bay, he lifted his arm and slowed. Luckily, there were three buoys left.

"Do you mind grabbing a bowline and tying us up?" he asked.

"I can handle that." She climbed up on the bow of the boat.

He groaned as he watched her climb across his boat in nothing but the tiniest pair of jean shorts and a white tank top with her hair pulled up in a messy bun. It had been years since he even allowed himself to view a woman as a sexual creature. That was his punishment for leaving his daughter with a drug addict to go meet his girlfriend.

He'd been a selfish prick.

It didn't matter that his marriage was over. Or that he and his wife hadn't been in a good place since their daughter had been three. If ever. He was a cheat and his family deserved better.

In his mind, he was just as at fault as his ex-wife.

But no one ever talked about that.

Tonya glanced over her shoulder and smiled. "All set."

"Thanks." He shut off the engine and offered her a hand. "Why don't we set up some towels on the stern and enjoy the sun for a bit, and then we can take a swim."

"Sounds refreshing." She helped him lay out a couple of beach towels over the back end of his boat, which really wasn't made for lounging, but they'd make do.

It was only ten in the morning, so he figured it was too early to pull out the wine. But he reached into the cooler and snagged two waters and a bowl of fruit. "I cut up some strawberries. I know how much you love them."

"Oh, my God." She dug in with her fingers and plopped a plump one in her mouth. "These are so good."

All he could see were her lips. And all he could think about was kissing them.

Thank God he'd kept his shades on so she had no idea he was staring at her mouth. But he had to wonder if she could hear his heart pounding against his chest. It beat so fast it hurt.

"This might be a stupid, silly question, but have you heard from Tiki and Lake?" he asked.

"I got a text from Tiki letting me know they got to the airport this morning. Their flight was at eight. She said she would let us know when they landed." Tonya twisted out of her shorts and shirt, revealing a tiny bikini.

"Wow," he managed. "Is that one of your sister's designs?"

"Fresh off the rack." Tonya smiled. "Although it's not this summer's line. She was playing around with some ideas for next year."

"It looks amazing on you." He glanced around at all the other boats as a rush of jealousy surged through his system. "What little there is of it."

"Trust me. There are ones that cover less. There is an entire line of thong bottoms this year and even the one-pieces are so revealing I couldn't possibly wear them. So many of them sold out, which is why she started on some of these. She said she might do a mid-season showing."

"While I like what I see, I wouldn't want you prancing around a beach or this bay in anything smaller, especially a thong."

She lowered her sunglasses and peered over the rims. "I don't know if I find that insulting or insanely sweet."

He chugged half his water, wishing it were a beer, before slipping off his shirt and tossing it to the seat.

"I've always been the kind of guy who prefers something a little more modest." He shrugged. "But I haven't been in this bay, or Sandy Bay, outside of wedding rides. I don't go to the beach. I'm never at a pool, so I have no idea what's in vogue when it comes to swimwear these days."

She laughed. The sound was like melting chocolate over his ears. For months, maybe even years, he'd been pushing down his attraction to Tonya, but he had no idea that when he let his guard down, it would completely crumble. The wall that he'd built around his emotions had been destroyed, leaving him vulnerable.

His therapist told him for a while now that he needed to put himself out there, but she told him to take it slowly.

He wasn't sure he'd be able to do that anymore. He couldn't deny the fact that he wanted Tonya. It wasn't only a physical thing. He cared for her deeply. His pulse raced.

"You act as though you've never seen me in a bathing suit."

He waved his finger up and down at her body. "I haven't seen you in something like that and I'm sorry that I'm acting like an idiot. You're incredibly beautiful and I'm having inappropriate thoughts."

"Thank you. I think." She leaned back, propping herself up on her elbows and lifting one knee.

"Do you have sunscreen on?" What a lame way of

asking to put his hands on her body.

"I do."

"Oh. Okay." He rolled to his stomach, keeping his weight on his forearms. "I wouldn't want you to burn." He ran his finger over her bare shoulder. Doug's words from last night rolled around in his mind. "I want to talk to you about something that might sour the mood a little bit, but I think it's necessary."

"That sounds serious."

"I feel like if we're going to try this dating thing, we need to discuss why I haven't even considered it since I left my wife."

She wadded up her cover-up and used it as a pillow, turning her head. "It's been seven years since you and Victoria divorced. Are you seriously going to tell me you haven't been out on a single date?"

"I don't expect anyone to understand, but no. I haven't. Not even a one-night stand."

"Are you telling me you haven't had sex since then?" Her cheeks turned a sweet blushing red.

God, he wanted to take her into his arms and kiss the hell out of her, but that would have to wait. "I know that seems strange, but I have my reasons."

"Seriously?" She lifted her sunglasses. "I just assumed like everything else, you kept all that private."

"You nailed one thing. If I had, I wouldn't shout it from the rooftops." His therapist was right about how talking openly with people he'd come to enjoy being around would feel good. Scary, but not totally out of his comfort zone. Especially with Tonya. "However, my reasons for remaining single, especially when it comes to having never acted on my growing attraction to you, are a cause for concern and something I want to address so you have all the facts."

"Foster. This isn't a business transaction."

"I know." He leaned in and pressed his lips against her warm skin. Right now, he wasn't sure if he should follow Doug's advice. Telling her might turn her off.

But if he didn't, and things blew up badly, he'd never forgive himself for not explaining how his mind and emotions worked.

"And I don't mean to sound that way. It's just that I don't ever want to hurt you, intentional or otherwise."

"Why are you worried about that?"

"Because I don't know if I can ever be in a forever kind of relationship, no matter how much I care for someone." Saying those words crushed his heart in ways he hadn't expected. It was like someone took a dagger and stabbed him, twisting and turning it until he bled out. "I certainly don't want to lead you on, but I can't deny that there is something wild, intense, and real between us."

She pushed herself up, sitting cross-legged. "This is just a first date."

He followed suit, facing her and taking her hands.

"When Lisa died, a piece of me went with her."

Tonya opened her mouth, but he hushed her by pressing a finger over her lips.

"You know I've spent years in therapy working really hard not to be this angry shell of a man. I'm trying to have a life, but even if I can get to the point where I want to be in a long-term relationship, I don't know that I can give you what you want and deserve."

"What is it that you think I want?"

"Marriage. Kids." His throat went dry the moment the latter word hit his lips. His heart raced, and not in a good way. His toes itched to feel a hard surface. The sudden urge to run overtook all the tender and warm feelings he had for Tonya.

And yet, a little voice in the back of his mind begged him to stay.

She lowered her gaze and fiddled with her thumbnail. "Perhaps those are things I want in the future. But you and I have barely started any kind of romantic relationship. Why are we discussing them now?"

"Because you need to know that I don't believe I can give you those things." He took her chin with his thumb and forefinger. "I've been denying my feelings for you for a long time and not just because I'm afraid that I can't do this. Living my life scares the crap out of me. Really starting my life over means I have to hold that mirror up and take a good look at who I am, and I haven't done that."

She palmed his cheek. "My grandfather has always told me that without risk, there is no reward."

"Your grandpa has a saying for everything."

"They are often true," she said. "We care about each other. If we don't try, we'll both wonder. Do you want that?"

"At this juncture, no." He brushed his lips over hers in a tender, slow kiss. She tasted like a mixture of strawberries and sunshine. It was intoxicating and he wasn't sure he could ever stop. "At the same time, I don't want to—"

"Stop," she whispered. "I appreciate what you're saying. But I don't need you to treat me with kid gloves. Let's enjoy the moment and see where this takes us."

"I'm so in over my head." He pulled her onto his lap, cradling her in his arms. He had no control over what he was feeling anymore. If he ended things right now, it would leave them both reeling, which wouldn't be healthy. Taking a leap of faith was his only option. Even if deep down, he believed his heart was broken and it would never mend to the point that he'd be whole.

Maybe it would be enough.

Perhaps he could pull himself into the present to the point he could be the kind of man Tonya deserved.

He took her mouth in a hot, passionate kiss. Totally improper for the surroundings. He had no idea who was watching, if anyone. And at this point, he didn't actually care. He'd forgotten how good it felt to have close human contact. He allowed himself to get lost in the moment.

Lost in Tonya.

Until he heard someone splashing in the water nearby.

"Foster? Is that you?" a female voice rang out.

He cringed. He knew that voice and he had never wanted to hear it again. The last time he had spoken to Kathy, it hadn't gone well. It never did. He dropped his forehead to Tonya's and took in a deep cleansing breath before he blinked open his eyes. He turned. "Hi, Kathy," he managed. Being niceish would be the only way to get through this awkward moment.

Kathy treaded in the water on the side of the boat with two other women. He recognized one of them as her cousin. He had no idea who the other one was and he didn't care.

"What are you doing here?" Kathy asked.

A sarcastic reply filled his mouth, but he swallowed it. Kathy could give as good as she got, and he wasn't ready to explain to Tonya his past relationship with Kathy. Though he probably should. However, this wasn't the right time or space.

"Enjoying a nice Sunday." He saw no need to elaborate any further. Kathy hadn't taken their breakup well. She desperately wanted to be there for him and comfort him in his time of grief. Or that's what she kept telling him, only her actions didn't match up with someone who understood what he had experienced. Kathy had been selfish and wanted the life she envisioned and that wasn't something he'd been capable of back then, much less with her.

While he never blamed Kathy for his daughter's death, she was the reason he'd been absent, and being around her was a constant reminder of his failure. Even now, it pulled up that pain, torturing his soul.

"I'm surprised to see you here with a lady," Kathy said. "Are you going to introduce me to your friend?"

Foster remembered the last time he saw Kathy. It had been six months ago when he'd been having lunch with Doug and Jim. He'd been working on a remodel project with them and they'd stopped at Jim's favorite sandwich shop. Kathy had been there picking up a to-go order.

She spent the last month texting him about how good he looked and how proud she was of him for getting his life back on track. He'd been kind and said thank you, but then came the message suggesting they get together. He'd been firm in his response, and again, she hadn't taken it well. She'd always felt they had unfinished business.

There was nothing left between them. He'd made that clear on several occasions.

"Tonya, this is Kathy." He leaned back on his hands, making sure one was behind Tonya's back, touching her hip, as if he were staking his claim, or perhaps just making sure that Kathy saw the physical contact.

"It's nice to meet you," Tonya said. Her voice had a slight twitch to it. That always happened when she was either uncomfortable or felt overwhelmed in any given situation.

"Likewise." Kathy smiled, but it wasn't the kind of smile that told someone they were happy to share the same space.

Kathy could cut someone to the bone when she felt backed into a corner or had been hurt. Foster had learned that the hard way. He honestly had thought she'd understand his need to be alone after the fire. That he couldn't be in a relationship with her after what happened, especially during the sentencing of Victoria.

"I heard that your wedding boat ride business is doing quite well." Kathy turned her focus to Foster.

"I'm booked all summer, mostly thanks to Tonya," he said proudly. "She's an amazing wedding and party planner. The best around town."

"Oh. You don't say. Does your business have a name?" Kathy asked.

"Events to Remember by Tonya Johnson," Tonya interjected.

"A friend of mine used you for a baby shower last summer. You do good work." Kathy glanced over her shoulder, waving to a bunch of people in a large cruiser. "Well, we better get back to our friends, but Foster, we should really get together sometime and catch up. We have some stuff to chat about."

"No, we don't." That flew out of his mouth quickly and with a touch of animosity laced in every word. He hadn't even thought about it, which he probably should have, but it was too late now.

Tonya lowered her chin, looking surprised by his abruptness.

"I'll be in touch." Kathy turned and swam off.

Thank God for small favors.

He had once cared a great deal for Kathy. However, she had been relentless in pursuing him after Lisa died. She wouldn't leave him alone or give him any space. She believed that all he needed was her love to get through his pain and grief.

What he'd said to her at the courthouse that day had to be some of the cruelest words he'd ever said to anyone. At the time, he'd meant them, but only because he was in so much pain. A few months later, he went to her and apologized. She took that as he wanted to get back together. The only language she understood was a firm tone.

"Who was that?" Tonya asked.

"Someone from my past." He let out a long breath. "I don't want to talk about her."

"No offense, but you were kind of mean to her."

Foster climbed into the boat, sitting in the second seat. He ran a hand over his mouth, running his index finger and thumb down his chin. He'd mentally prepared himself for a lot of things today.

A few intense and passionate kisses.

Warm embraces.

Cuddling.

Perhaps some uncomfortable yet necessary conversations.

His mind had played a million possible scenarios of how today could play out, but none included running into Kathy, of all people. He had no idea how to process the encounter or what to do with the emotions seeing her brought up.

Tonya joined him, keeping her gaze hyper-focused on him, and it rattled his nerves.

He didn't want to get into this now.

"I'm sorry that I was rude," he said.

"It's not me you should apologize to."

He turned, looking Tonya in the eye. "That's not going to happen. If I do that, she'll hound me."

"She's an ex-girlfriend? But you said you didn't date after you divorced Victoria."

"I haven't dated anyone in seven years," he said.

Tonya narrowed her stare, then slowly her eyes grew wide. "You were cheating on Victoria," she whispered. She took her cover-up and wrapped it around her body.

That spoke volumes.

So much for a great first date.

5

onya folded her arms across her middle and sank into the plush high-end vinyl cushions. She stared at the bright-blue sky. In the distance, one of the boats played an upbeat country music song. She resisted the urge to tap her toes while she waited for an explanation.

Five minutes passed.

Then ten.

It amazed her how he could sit in an uncomfortable silence and appear like he didn't have a care in the world.

"Are we going to talk about what just happened?" she asked.

"Obviously, I'd rather not." He pushed his sunglasses up his nose.

"You know I'm not a judgmental person."

"You are when it comes to this." He turned. "And

I understand why. What Josh did to your sister was a dick move, and I'm very aware of how my actions affected my family." He stuffed the strawberry container into the cooler and folded up his towel.

"I know your marriage wasn't a good one and—"

"I don't want to talk about this," Foster said sharply. He leaned into the cockpit and turned the key before climbing to the bow and releasing the boat from the buoy.

She sighed. "We don't have to leave."

"I'm sorry, but this is one of the many reasons I didn't want to do this." He maneuvered the boat between other vessels as he left Paradise Bay and made his way into open waters. "This was a bad idea."

"Wait a second." She reached across his body, putting her hand over his, preventing him from pressing the throttle down. "I need you to be clear. Is dating in general a bad idea? Or are you just sour because we ran into Kathy?"

"Both," he admitted. "Now, please drop it. I'm not in the mood."

"I think you're full of shit." She lifted her legs and rested them on the side. "You're avoiding where things were going so you're using the fact that I got a little weirded out by something in your past that I didn't know about, which by the way, if you gave me half a chance and let me, I might actually be understanding."

"And maybe this has nothing to do with any of that and I just don't want to talk about it and have come to the conclusion that it's time this day ends." He brought the boat to full speed.

She kept her focus on the shoreline and her tears to herself.

Better to find out sooner rather than later.

Hopefully, the tension would dissipate by the time they reached his dock, but it didn't. If anything, it got worse. Foster had retreated so deeply inside himself that he wasn't coming out anytime soon.

It had been a long time since she'd seen him like this and she didn't like it.

"Let me take that." Foster took the cooler from her hands and set it on the wood planks, helping her disembark.

She followed him up the path to the driveway. Opening the trunk of her car, she tossed her belongings in the back.

He stood a few paces away with his hands in his pockets and a guilty look on his face, reminding her that he'd cheated on his wife instead of filing for divorce, something that he'd thought about doing for years, but didn't. He thought Victoria would end up dead because of her addiction, leaving their daughter without a mother.

"I'll see you later," he said.

She wanted to force the issue, her grandfather's voice prodding in the back of her head, telling her to push him to talk. That he needed to stop hiding. But more so that she needed to ask him to do that for her —for them.

But she couldn't.

Not in this moment.

"Call me if you want to." She slipped behind the steering wheel and drove off with her heart in her gut.

She'd known Foster was a complicated man with a difficult past. She had no idea how heartbreaking it would be to love him.

Foster strolled down the alleyway with a couple of bags. He paused in front of Victoria's things, but still no Victoria. He turned. "Have you seen her?" he asked Tony.

"Yes." Tony took the water bottle that Foster offered. "She was here for a couple of hours last night. She's limping real bad."

"Did you ask her what happened?" Foster wanted to go through her things, but he knew if he did that, he'd get attacked by some of the other homeless. They might not look like much, but they had a wicked sense of community and some didn't like or trust him, thanks to things that Victoria had said.

"She told me to mind my own fucking business."

Foster chuckled. "Sounds like Victoria."

"I'm worried about her," Tony said. "She doesn't

seem right."

"Does anyone around here have access to a phone?"

"We can use the convenience store phone in an emergency."

"Please have someone reach out to me." Foster pulled out another card and handed it to Tony. "I want to know when she comes back. Maybe she needs medical attention."

"I'll try." Tony nodded.

"Here. Share this between you and Victoria." He placed the bags on the pavement.

"You're a very kind man." Tony rubbed his scruffy face. "Even though Victoria says you're evil."

Foster made his way back to the Blue Moon. He entered the bar, ordered a bourbon, and made his way to the terrace where he found a seat overlooking the lake.

"Hello," a male voice said. "My name is Maverick Snow. These are my brothers, Nelson and Phoenix. We're the owners of the Blue Moon. We've seen you in here a few times and we wanted to introduce ourselves."

Foster stood, stretching out his arm. "The name's Foster. It's nice to meet you."

"Don't you work for Sutten and Tanner?" Maverick asked. "And are the wedding driver?"

"I do." Foster nodded. "And I am."

"Doug and Jim did a great job for us," Nelson

said. "We thought you looked more familiar than just hanging out at the bar. Please let us know if there's anything we can personally do for you."

Phoenix pointed to the drink. "Next one's on the house."

"Thanks. I appreciate it," Foster said.

"Say hello to Doug and Jim for us." Maverick smiled. He and his brothers meandered around the patio, greeting the guests.

Foster sat back down and sighed. His mind had been playing the same loop all day and he couldn't shut it down.

Even as he stared at the dark night, his mind saw a blazing fire with tall, burning fingers reaching for the sky, carrying his precious daughter to heaven.

That is if you believed in that kind of thing.

"Foster? What are you doing here?" Lake asked.

"Oh. Hey." Foster waved at the empty chair next to him. "Care to join me for a drink?"

"I'm here with my sister, Brandi. She's up from New York City to discuss some publishing things. She leaves tomorrow."

Foster chuckled. "Looks like she's flirting with one of the owners of this fine establishment."

Lake glanced over his shoulder. "Shit," he mumbled. "That explains a lot."

"What does?"

"I couldn't figure out why we couldn't just walk down to the Mason Jug for a drink and discuss business. Or even do it at the house. But she had to come here. She's been obsessed with this place since we came here the last time she was visiting."

"That's the first time I met the owners," Foster said. "I thought they were going to rely more on their management team to run this place."

"I think one of the brothers is going to run the show." Lake eased into the chair and crossed his legs. "I suppose I should find out more if my sister is going to be coming up here regularly and using business as the excuse."

Foster laughed.

"So, why are you here, alone?" Lake arched a brow.

"Went on a hunt for Victoria." In the last year, Foster had gotten relatively close to Lake and Gael. He considered them friends. Good friends. He'd shared with them some of his history. At least the parts that most people knew. The fire had been public record. Everyone who had lived in the area knew he lost his daughter. Those facts he couldn't deny. He went a few steps deeper as he did his best to develop stronger bonds with humans. But now, he had to skate on thin ice. Anything he said could find its way back to Tonya. He didn't want her to feel as though he was speaking behind her back or discussing their personal business with everyone else.

"How is she?" Lake asked.

"Haven't seen her in a while, and I've been told

she might be hurt."

"You know where to find me if you ever need help."

"Thanks," Foster said.

"How was your date?"

Foster lifted his drink and took two big gulps. It went down smooth as butter, but his heart, his soul, and his brain were not all on the same page.

"I'm sure Tonya will say something to Tiki so I guess it's safe to say it sucked, but it was all my fault." He tilted his head. "Well, not entirely, but I let someone from my past ruin it, and now I don't think I can repair the damage."

Lake laughed.

"I'm not sure why that's funny."

"Because you're so dramatic and full of shit. Of course, things can be fixed. It can't be that bad."

Foster pinched the bridge of his nose. His dirty little secret was going to get out. Hell, it was out in so many circles.

His mother knew.

Victoria knew.

Her parents knew.

But he wasn't sure if anyone else did. He'd been lucky it had been kept out of the media and no one ever brought it up.

Except Kathy was his constant reminder.

"Oh. It's bad," Foster said. "The woman I was having an affair with when Lisa died showed up on our date. I didn't know what to say or do, so I acted like an asshole and we went home. End of story." He downed the rest of his drink, grateful the waiter brought over his complementary one, along with Lake's drink.

"Holy shit." Lake leaned forward, sipping his beverage. "You really are into self-sabotage."

"That's not a helpful comment."

"But it's the truth."

Foster couldn't argue the point.

"Tonya's a reasonable woman." Lake said. "Probably the most pragmatic of the three sisters. Not that any of them can condone cheating, but we can all see where there might be a set of circumstances that—"

"Trust me, I've justified my actions, but there's more to this story, and the person I need to have this conversation with is Tonya." Even if she didn't forgive Foster for his past bad behavior or how he treated her earlier, he owed her an apology and an explanation.

"I'm glad you realize that."

Foster glanced at his watch. "It's too late tonight and I've got work early, but hopefully she'll hear me out tomorrow."

"I'm sure she will." Lake stood. "I better go save Nelson from my sister before she eats him alive."

Foster decided to stay a little while longer and enjoy his drink along with the view, while going over in his mind all the things he planned on saying to Tonya.

6

Tonya sat at her kitchen table, staring at her computer, but she was unable to concentrate on work all day. Yesterday hadn't gone as planned.

It started great. She had felt confident, and Foster had been sweet and romantic. He'd opened up to her about his fears and concerns. She understood his vulnerability and respected his boundaries.

However, she'd struggled to get past the situation with Kathy.

It wasn't just that he'd cheated on his wife and that in all the years she'd been friends with Foster, that was something she hadn't known. Of course, she figured there were many things about him that would be revealed to her as they got to know each other in a different, more intimate way.

But never in a million years would she have

expected Foster to be the kind of man who would step out of his marriage.

She tried to remind herself how bad his relationship had been. Victoria had been doing heroin when she accidentally set the house on fire that killed their daughter, and almost killed herself. Foster had mentioned more than once that his ex-wife had checked out and that he was already thinking about divorce, but he had a daughter to consider, and she was his top priority.

Sleeping with another woman didn't live up to that statement and Tonya struggled with her personal standards.

But it was the way in which Foster closed himself off that upset her the most. He hadn't even given them a chance to discuss it.

Her cell buzzed.

Foster: *Are you home?*

She let out a sigh. She hadn't reached out to Foster since their date. He'd texted her four times, asking if they could talk and she hadn't responded yet.

Was she ready to listen to what he had to say now?

Tonya: *Yes.*

She stared at her phone, waiting for the three little bubbles to appear. Thirty seconds passed.

Nothing.

A minute.

Still, no bubbles. No text.

She tossed her cell back onto the table.

A tap at the door startled her and she knocked over her glass. Thank goodness it was empty and it didn't shatter. She picked it up off the floor and set it on the counter before scurrying to the front door where she peered through the window.

Foster stood there with a pizza box and a six-pack.

She twisted the handle and let him in.

"I took a chance you might be hungry and willing to talk to me," he said. "You've ignored me most of the day."

"I've been busy, but I'm starving, so I'll accept your food." She took the beer from his hand, taking two out and sticking the rest in the fridge. She cleared her stuff off the table and pulled down two plates while her heart hammered in the center of her chest.

"I owe you an apology for my behavior yesterday." He lifted a slice and put it on one of the plates. "And I want to explain some things."

"I can understand not wanting to talk, but you shut down completely. Gave up altogether. That wasn't fair." She tore off a piece of crust and nibbled, leaning back in her chair. This had been one of those situations she wished she could talk to someone about, but she couldn't because this was Foster's private business. She wouldn't do that to him. That part of his life had been incredibly painful and for her to discuss it with someone, even one of her sisters, wouldn't be cool. "Nor is expecting me to hear you out on your terms as if I'm sitting around waiting for you."

However, that left her stewing in a million questions.

"I shouldn't have ambushed you this way, but I've been working with Doug and Jim all day right down the street and I didn't want to let this simmer. I don't want to ruin something just as it was getting off the ground."

"I would have reached out eventually."

"Well, you didn't do anything wrong, so it shouldn't be up to you to come to me. I want to tell you about what happened with Kathy." He held her gaze.

"I'm listening."

"I'm not proud of the fact I cheated on my wife. There is no excuse for what I did. I tried to justify it in my mind that we were miserable and didn't have much of a marriage, but I was a selfish prick for what I did."

"Putting myself in your shoes, I can understand your actions." She held up her hand. "I don't agree with them; however, I'm not condemning them either. I'm simply sensitive to the cheating thing because of what happened to Tiki and I wouldn't want someone to do that to me."

"I have a few regrets in life, and being with Kathy is one of them." He took a long swig of his beer. His eyes glossed over. "It's not just the guilt of having an affair because while I was in it, I only worried about Lisa. What it would do to her if what her father was doing ever came out. I honestly didn't consider Victoria's feelings. We hadn't slept in the same bed in years. We had no relationship except for the fact that I took care of her and that often infuriated me. Sometimes I think I used Kathy to get back at Victoria for choosing drugs over her child."

"Can I ask you something?" Tonya had been thinking about this all day. She wasn't sure if she'd be able to gain the courage to ask the tough questions. She cared for Foster and she wanted the chance to see if they could move past the friend zone.

No risk. No reward.

If she stayed passive in her role when it came to defining their relationship, she'd forever be lonely. And that would be true with any man she dated.

"Of course."

"Why are you so angry with Kathy? And yourself, because I heard something in your voice that I don't hear very often. It was this deep sense of loathing."

He took his beer and stood, making his way to the window that overlooked the parking area.

While she had access to the waterfront, her carriage house didn't have a view of the lake. She didn't mind, though. Just being able to sit at the docks was enough. For now. She dreamed of someday living next to her parents, in her grandfather's house. Although that thought hurt her soul because it meant her grandpa would no longer be with her, and also if her dream was with Foster, it wouldn't be in that house.

She continued to eat her pizza while she patiently waited for Foster to find the words. One thing she understood about him was that he took his time when it came to important answers.

"I don't know if I can ever get past this part." He turned, leaning against the wall between the sofa and the front door. "I was with Kathy when I got the call my house was on fire."

Tonya dropped her slice of pizza in her lap. She covered her mouth and gasped. So many things about Foster made sense with that one sentence.

He swiped at his eyes before pushing off the wall and strolling across the room. Setting his beer down, he lifted the slice off her lap and began cleaning off the saucy, cheesy mess.

She was too stunned to move, much less say anything.

Taking her hands, he lifted his gaze. "I don't think I have to tell you why I still struggle with my actions the night Lisa died. I left my beautiful little girl with a drug addict so I could go be with another woman. What kind of man—father—does that make me?"

She palmed his cheek. "A human one."

He kissed the back of her hand. "That's kind of you, but based on your reaction yesterday, and even a few seconds ago, you think I'm a snake."

"Don't you dare put words in my mouth." She waggled her finger.

He arched a brow. "I would have some harsh words for me."

"I'm not going to sit here and judge you. I know the hell your ex-wife has put you through and I have a better understanding why you have so much guilt. That's a lot to carry around."

"If I hadn't gone to see Kathy that night, my little girl would still be alive."

Tonya's heart hurt. She understood why he pulled everything back to that one decision. His decision. However, he wasn't to blame. His indiscretion didn't cause the fire. "How many times did you catch Victoria asleep on the sofa or in her room with a lit cigarette?"

"Too many times to count and that wasn't the first time a fire had been started, but that's not the point."

"Foster, it's exactly the point. I know you hate it when people say this, but you're not to blame." For years, she had avoided using those words because it got under his skin to the point he'd often tell people that until they lived his life, they had no idea where blame or guilt could be placed. She even once heard him tell a friend to fuck off over it.

"I wasn't there because I chose to be selfish. That's a fact that can't be changed and something that I live with every day. Therapy has helped me understand that I'm not responsible for Victoria's actions. For her choices. For her addiction. However, no matter how hard I try, I can't erase that gut-wrenching feeling that all I had to do was not make that one decision."

Telling him that it wasn't that simple wasn't going to ease his pain. She wasn't sure anything would.

"I'm sorry, Foster. But you're wrong. I won't disagree that perhaps you were selfish. Looking back, you could have done things differently, but that doesn't change the fact that Victoria was a drug addict and she did things that put Lisa in harm's way."

"But I shouldn't have allowed her to be alone—"

"You didn't. Victoria took Lisa without your permission more than once, right?"

Foster nodded.

"She manipulated babysitters. She snuck out in the middle of the night. And bad things happened right under your nose." Tonya blinked out a tear. "I know you will always have these emotions. I accept that, but you have to stop drowning in them."

"I know, but seeing Kathy doesn't make it easy."

"Why do you harbor such resentment toward her? I'm sorry if I'm making it a bigger deal than it needs to be, but I was surprised by the venom in your tone."

"It's all part of the reasons why I am the way I am, especially in regard to dating." He lifted her from the seat and guided her toward the sofa. "However, it is a complicated answer."

"I'm listening." She tucked her feet under her butt.

"Kathy and I weren't seeing each other that long. I'd made it clear to her that my daughter would always be my priority. But I got caught up in feeling alive. And like a man again. It was exciting and when she called or texted, my heart raced and I wanted to be with her. The longer the affair lasted, the more risks I took. Part of me wanted to get caught because maybe then I could end my marriage, which both my mother and Victoria's parents begged me to do. No one believed it was healthy for anyone, including Lisa."

"Why didn't you divorce Victoria?"

"Guilt," he said. "Addiction is a disease. One she doesn't have control over when she's using. When we would fight and I'd bring up separating, she'd threaten to kill herself."

"That's emotional blackmail."

Foster nodded. "I know. But then I'd tuck our daughter in at night and think about what it would be like to have to tell her that her mother was dead. It brought tears to my eyes every time. Not to mention how much Lisa loved her mother. There were these moments when Victoria would be somewhat present and would play dolls or board games with Lisa. In those times, I couldn't bring myself to do it. I'd tell myself when Lisa was older. When she had developed more and understood more about her mother's illness.

She had already started asking questions. I figured it was only a matter of time. I also was still holding out hope that Victoria would get help. She had periods where she would stay clean, and she would promise me she was going to change. It never lasted."

A thick lump formed in Tonya's throat. She couldn't imagine the hell that Foster lived all those years. And to carry around the burden still today.

"I found some comfort with Kathy and a little normalcy. I cared for her. A lot. She was with me when I got that call. I asked her to stay away from the hospital, but she came anyway. We had a fight in the parking lot. I have no idea how the media never caught wind of our affair, and I will forever be grateful to her for not exposing it, because she could have. She threatened to enough times. I believe she didn't because of her career and how it could make her look."

"That makes her a coldhearted person if you believe she wasn't doing it to protect you and your family."

"Trust me, that wasn't on Kathy's mind. She had a different agenda and making either one of us look bad didn't fit her plans," Foster said. "I ended things right there. I told her I could never be with her again. I did say I didn't blame her. That it wasn't her fault and that I wanted us to go our separate ways with as little hurt as possible. She wouldn't accept that answer. She was relentless in her pursuit of me for two years.

It got so bad that I threatened to file a restraining order. That's when she backed off until recently."

"What do you mean?" Tonya pulled a chunk of hair over her shoulder and twisted it between her fingers. "Have you been talking with her? Or did you have lunch or something?"

"Nothing like that." He smiled. "Anyone ever tell you that you're cute when you're jealous?"

"No. And I'm not," she said. "Okay. Maybe a little."

He rested his hand on her thigh and squeezed. "Long story short. I ran into her and she started reaching out again. I'm not sure why she's hell-bent on bringing up the past or why she believes we have any unfinished business. And just to be totally transparent, she's texted me twice today."

"Have you responded?" Tonya had no right to ask. It wasn't any of her business. This was between Foster and an ex. It had nothing to do with Tonya.

He took her chin with his thumb and forefinger. "No. I have no desire to have any kind of conversation with Kathy. Not now. Not ever."

"Do you think she's looking for closure?" Tonya understood how important that was to most people. She hadn't many long-term relationships, but the few she did have, that was something that helped her move forward. "I don't mean to be rude or insensitive, but you did close yourself off to the world for a while."

"You're right. I did. However, for an entire year, I kept telling her that I had nothing to give. I was a shell of a man who'd lost his only child. She pushed and she pushed and she pushed until I lost my shit and told her that if she didn't leave me alone, I'd take action."

"I'm sure that hurt her feelings, especially if she thought there was any chance that the two of you were going to make a life together."

Foster inhaled sharply and exhaled with a big sigh. "She never even met my daughter. There was no talk of us staying together. It wasn't that I hadn't thought about it, because I did care about Kathy, but I wasn't in a position that I felt comfortable leaving Victoria." He pinched the bridge of his nose. "If she believed that, it didn't come from me."

"I'm sorry. I'm not trying to make you defensive. I'm only trying to understand."

"I know," he whispered. "It just brings up a lot of emotions and all the reasons that I never allowed myself to really let you in. I knew if I did, I'd not only answer any question you wanted to know, but I'd have to look it all in the face. Even in therapy, I can be somewhat emotionless. It's hard to do that with you now that we've expressed that there's something between us."

"I'm not sure I get how that's connected to me."

"I was never in love with Victoria. Not like a man should love a woman. She was the mother of my child

87

and I valued that and loved her for giving me Lisa. I couldn't ever take that away from Victoria, but we should have never gotten married in the first place. We were both pressured to do so because Victoria was pregnant. When I met Kathy, I wasn't looking for anything. I was half-dead inside. I was doing my best to be a good father. I failed."

"That's not true."

He ran his hand up and down her leg, massaging gently. "But it is. I try not to place all the blame on myself. I accept that there were things beyond my control; however, I made some pretty big mistakes that I have to take responsibility for. The thing is, after Kathy, I decided that my punishment should be to live out my life alone, because if I ever let another woman in, that meant I was betraying my daughter's memory."

She tapped the center of her chest. Her eyes filled with tears. "I don't want you to feel that way about me."

"That's the hard part. I don't," he said. "I care about you. I thought I could brush it under the rug. But I can't. So, shall we try another date next Sunday?"

"Tonight could be a date." She lifted her thumb to her mouth and chewed on her nail.

"I hate it when you do that." He pushed her hand from her face. "What do you have in mind?"

"That new action flick just dropped on streaming.

We could make some popcorn and watch it together. I know we watch television all the time, but it could be one way to ease back into things."

"I like the sound of that." He leaned closer, brushing his mouth over her lips. A soft, tender kiss that left her weak in the knees.

It ended way too quickly.

However, the night was still young.

Foster couldn't concentrate on the movie, which made him crazy because it wasn't like he'd never forced himself to focus on something other than Tonya. However, this time she was snuggling up against him, her skin touching his, reminding him that she was all woman, and he indeed was a man. He glanced down at the head resting in his lap. He ran his fingers through Tonya's long dark locks. Eerie music echoed through the room, followed by the boom of drums as the bad guys broke down a door.

She jumped, grabbing his thighs.

He chuckled.

"Not funny." She glanced up. "This wasn't supposed to be a scary movie."

"I believe it's advertised as suspense, but it has a horror flare." He ran his hand up and down her arm. "We don't have to continue watching if you don't want to."

"If you're enjoying it, we can."

"I've been a bit distracted. I'm a little lost, so I kind of have no idea what's going on."

"Why aren't you paying attention?" She scooted to her knees, tucking her feet under her adorable ass.

His pulse raced. For years he'd been comfortably numb. It wasn't that he was void of emotion. It was more that he swallowed them, keeping them in a box in his soul. He'd gotten good at existing. However, now that he'd tasted Tonya, he wanted more. "All I can think about is you."

"Oh." Her lips curled into a smile. Her cheeks flushed.

He reached out and tucked a few stray strands of hair behind her ear. In the years that he'd known Tonya, he never allowed himself to think about his attraction. If he did, he would find ways to occupy his hands and his mind. He had to admit that in recent months it had become harder and harder, but until Tiki and Lake's wedding, he could pretend Tonya wasn't interested. Therefore, neither was he.

"And what exactly are you thinking?"

He arched a brow. "I'm not sure I want to tell you."

"Why not?"

"I don't want to get slapped."

Laughing, she straddled his lap, resting her hands on his shoulders. "Whatever's going on in your mind seems a hell of a lot more interesting than that movie."

He swallowed.

Hard.

This was moving fast, though he thought it might. Doug warned him it would and even suggested it was best to dive right in.

Her lips came crashing down on his mouth before he could manage another word, or even another thought.

He gripped her hips, holding her steady, not wanting her to move. He couldn't handle the pressure. It had been seven years since he'd been with a woman. Up until this moment, he hadn't missed it. He told himself he could live out the rest of his life without female companionship. Had Tonya never come into his world the way she had, he probably could have, but she changed everything.

She was soft and sweet and kind. She made him want to be the best version of himself that he could be. Even when she hadn't made her feelings known and he was still pretending he didn't have any emotions, he still tried harder when he was in her presence.

His heart pounded in his chest, dropping to his toes and thrusting up to his brain like a rocket.

Taking him by the hands, she stood, tugging him across the family room and toward the hallway.

"Hey," he managed. "I don't have any protection

with me. I wasn't even sure you'd see me."

"Good thing I have condoms."

He coughed. The Tonya he'd known all these years tended to be on the shyer side. Or at least that's what he expected her to be when it came to the affairs of the heart because she'd never expressed her attraction.

"Too bold?" She paused midstep.

"Would it have been worse if I brought them with me? Not that I've bought them in years." Jesus, that sounded pathetic. "I'm making this insanely awkward."

She dropped her head to his chest and wrapped her arms around his waist. "Do you know how many people don't have the conversation?"

"Actually, I have a good idea." He lifted her chin with his forefinger. "How about we stop talking altogether and take this to your bedroom?" He licked his lips before kissing hers. It lasted only a few seconds, but it was powerful. It twisted his stomach into knots. It made him light-headed.

They stumbled down the hallway and into her small bedroom which barely had room for a queen-sized bed.

At least he assumed that was the size since it wasn't as big as his bed in his loft. But he didn't care.

A bed was a bed and they didn't need that much space.

He lifted his shirt over his head, tossing it across

the room before grappling at the buttons on her blouse. It was as if he'd never taken off a woman's clothing before.

She batted his hands away and swiftly removed her top. Her bra. And her jeans.

Taking a step back, he stared at her beautiful body, wondering how he ended up in this space and time. Again, he'd never allowed his mind to even fantasize about her. When he took care of himself, he thought about—or looked at—women who didn't exist. He could never pull it into the real world. That would make him human.

"Wow," he whispered. He shouldn't stand there and stare, but he couldn't take his eyes off her. His fingers itched to touch her silky skin.

He shed the rest of his clothing and pulled her close. While he'd forgotten what it felt like to hold a woman, none of that mattered. The only thing he cared about was making sure he could satisfy Tonya. This should be like riding a bike, but seven years was a fucking long time.

"Right back at you." Her warm lips pressed against the center of his chest. Her hands roamed his body.

He tried to find his voice to tell her to stop, or to at least slow down, but he couldn't. And he wasn't entirely sure he wanted to either. Everything about her felt so damn good.

So fucking wild and out of control.

He'd spent the last few years of his life barely living. Or perhaps living vicariously through other people. While he personally never experienced true love, he one hundred percent believed in it. That's why he created his wedding driver business. He enjoyed being on the fringe of happiness, but not in the thick of it. Right now, the blood in his veins pumped so hot he thought he might explode. It was the closest he'd come to pure joy since the birth of his daughter.

Fisting her hair, he stared at her as she kissed her way down his stomach. His breath caught in the center of this throat. Sex with Victoria had become nonexistent after a few years of marriage. He didn't ask for it and she didn't offer. It had been easy to go without. He didn't care until he'd met Kathy. Then it had become exciting again.

He had a life outside of his daughter and that was thrilling in ways he couldn't describe. When it all went up in smoke—literally—the passion in his heart died.

Tonya breathed life into his soul.

Groaning, he did his best to maintain composure. The last thing he wanted to do was lose control and have this encounter end before it even got off the ground.

Tonya's sexual desire had been unexpected. Mind-blowing. Every time he thought about taking over, he gave up. Whatever she wanted, he had to give her, and the most important was pleasure.

His mind filled with worry that he'd forgotten what to do, but based on her sweet, soft moans and the way her fingers threaded through his hair, he was hitting all the right marks. Her hips ground against the roll of his tongue. She tasted like strawberry jam on warm country bread.

Listening to her whisper his name as her climax built excited him more than the idea she was about to be pushed over the edge and he would be responsible for that most exquisite kind of satisfaction. He wouldn't care if he had an orgasm as long she had one that made her body shiver in delight.

"Yes. Yes. Oh, my God, Foster, yes."

He pressed his hand over her stomach. It quivered under his touch. He kissed his way up to her breasts, sucking each nipple into his mouth, making sure he gave attention to each one. He found the box of condoms and fumbled like a stupid teenager.

Gritting his teeth, he entered her in one long, torturous stroke. He wasn't sure he'd last longer than a few more, so he took it slow, easing in and out as if there was no urgency, until she gripped his ass, encouraging him to go deep and hard.

It took maybe a minute before his release collided inside of Tonya, mixing with hers in a cosmic meeting of epic proportions. He honestly didn't think he'd ever experienced anything so powerful. Or magical. He'd never be able to put into words what he felt in this moment.

He couldn't catch his breath as he rolled to the side, pulling the covers over their naked bodies. His chest rose as he tried to fill his lungs, but it wasn't enough. Wrapping a protective arm around Tonya, he pulled her close. He blinked.

This changed everything.

Fear gripped his heart.

Panic seeped into his mind.

Living a little was one thing. Doing it with Tonya could only lead to him breaking her heart. That was the last thing he wanted to do.

She snuggled in, resting her head on his chest. Her skin felt like a warm blanket. Part of him wanted to climb out of bed and run as fast and far away as he could.

But that wouldn't solve anything.

"This might not be the right moment, but you're welcome to spend the night," she whispered, running her fingers across his chest.

He pressed his lips against her temple. "I wasn't planning on leaving." Not entirely true, but he couldn't hurt her feelings and he honestly didn't want to get out of bed, put his clothes on, and make his way outside. He might as well stay put. "Although, I do have to get up early, so I'll try not to wake you."

"No worries if you do." She yawned. "Good night, Foster."

"Sleep well, Tonya."

oster rummaged through the kitchen as quietly as possible while he found a mug and made himself a cup of coffee.

"Foster? Are you still here?" Tonya's voice rang out soft and sweet.

"In the kitchen," he said. "I'm sorry if I woke you. I tried to be quiet and I hope you don't mind that I took a shower."

"Not at all." She appeared wearing nothing but a tank top and boy shorts. He tried not to stare, but it was impossible. "My internal clock goes off every morning at this time." She reached up, opened the cabinet, and pulled down a mug, putting it under the coffee machine. Her shirt lifted, showing off her firm midriff. Waking up with her arms sprawled out over his torso had been the purist form of torture.

In both a good and bad way.

He wanted more of her, and yet he couldn't bring himself to dare ask for it. If he'd been more emotionally available and less cut off from the world, maybe he could have; however, for now, he needed to slow down. To take a breath.

"Can I make you something to eat before you take off?"

"Doug and Jim always have something on-site." He raised his mug. "But I might make a second one of these. Do you have a travel mug I can borrow?"

"I sure do." She took two steps and rummaged through a different cabinet before turning. "This should do the trick. Shall I fill it for you?"

He peered inside his current beverage. Three-quarters full and now that she was awake and the jobsite was only a quarter mile away, he wasn't in such a hurry to leave. "Not yet." He set his drink on the counter and inched closer. His heart beat in the center of his throat. Part of him really wanted to be a different kind of man. If he could only mend what was broken inside his soul. If he could figure out how to do that, maybe he could be what she needed. "Good morning." He gripped her hips.

Smiling, she tilted her head. "I thought you snuck out."

"I was trying to be nice and let you sleep. The sun isn't even over the mountains yet."

"I appreciate that." She raised up on tiptoes, pressing her breasts against his chest.

He groaned.

"But next time you slip out of bed in the morning, you can kiss me goodbye. If it's not time for me to get up, I'll doze back off."

"I'll keep that in mind." He brushed his mouth over her sweet lips. It was like kissing a piece of candy.

"Do you have plans tonight?"

He chuckled. That was like asking a monk if he had a girlfriend. However, this was his busy season. "I have a dusk wedding cruise, and then I wanted to check on Victoria."

"I could help you find her." Tonya twisted, snagging her coffee.

"I haven't seen her in a few days. It could take a while, so I don't want to drag you around." Foster tried to do a visual check on Victoria at least twice a month. It had been about a week now since he'd seen her last and he was concerned about her health.

"I don't mind."

He cupped her chin. "I know. But I'll already be in the village. And then I have a little grocery shopping to do."

"What does the rest of your week look like?"

"Three dusk weddings." He kissed her nose. "Thursday is your client."

"That's right." She nodded. "You've got a busy week."

He lifted his mug and finished the coffee before

taking the to-go one and putting it under the machine. "I do."

"Would you be interested in getting together with Tayla and Gael this weekend? They've been bugging me and truthfully, the idea of being a third wheel is not appealing."

He laughed. "Sure. Either Friday or Saturday is fine. Just make it after six, okay?"

"Will do."

He pulled her in for one last embrace and kissed her forehead. "I'll talk to you later."

"Have a good day," she said as if this were a normal morning.

He stepped out into the warm summer morning. The sun peeked out over the mountain, barely lighting the sky. He'd always loved mornings. They were the most peaceful part of the day and full of promise. But after his daughter died, he resented them.

They were another constant reminder that he had to suffer through another day without his darling Lisa. He'd rather enjoy the evening where he knew he'd be closing his eyes and perhaps the one person he loved the most would visit him in his dreams.

The sound of rubber scuffing the pavement caught his attention. He turned his head toward the lake.

Jared and his oldest daughter, Caitlyn.

"Good morning, Foster," Jared said. "I'm surprised to see you here."

Foster glanced over his shoulder at the carriage house. He wasn't quite sure what to say. His daughter was in college, but still, he was leaving a woman's home bright and early. That generally only meant one thing.

"Are you really, Dad?" Caitlyn asked with a grin. "You and Mom both commented last night when you saw his car here how thrilled you were."

Jared tilted his head and arched a brow.

If Foster were his kid, he'd be running for the hills right about now based on that look.

"What?" Caitlyn gave the look right back at her father. "That's what you said."

Jared tossed his keys toward his oldest child, who had to be close to twenty at this point. "Get in the car, if you want to go see your boyfriend before I ask to have him transferred across the state."

"You wouldn't dare."

"Then stop testing me because as I told you last night, I'm in no mood." Jared pointed toward his truck. "Now go."

"Fine." Caitlyn shook her head. "What good is being an adult if I still get treated like a child," she mumbled.

Jared sucked in a deep breath and closed his eyes until the roar of his engine turned over. "I promised my wife I wouldn't lose my temper with her this morning. I want to know what happened to my sweet baby girl who thought her daddy was the bomb."

Foster laughed. "Sorry. I shouldn't find that funny."

"She's so much like me it's nuts. Stubborn as all get-out and she digs her heels into the ground just like I do. I know at the end of the day she understands, but she's so pissed because all of her friends are going on this trip for a week, but her boyfriend is doing an internship at my station and I can't give him the time off or he won't get the credits he needs. She doesn't seem to understand why, even though Calvin does. He didn't even ask me; she did. She doesn't comprehend I can't bend the rules just because of her." Jared leaned against the fence by the parking area near the carriage house. "I gave him a long weekend, but that's not good enough for my daughter, and my thinking is she should be damn grateful that we're letting her go away at all considering her attitude. It's tough because I like her boyfriend. He's going to make a great state trooper and I hope he asks to be at my station because I'd fight for him."

"That puts you between a rock and a hard place."

"Tell me about it," Jared said. "Sorry she called you out. That feistiness she gets from her mother, but that's no excuse for her embarrassing you to get to me."

"Don't worry about it." Foster never got to that stage with Lisa. When she died, she was still the apple of her father's eye. She would race to the door to throw her arms around her daddy when he came home from work. He could do no wrong and she loved him with all her heart.

He loved her more, but he'd failed her miserably.

Jared was the best parent Foster had ever met. His kids were generally quite respectful and didn't get into any trouble.

Well, nothing too horrible.

"I've seen her and Calvin a few times at the pizza joint in town. They make a cute couple," Foster said. "Young love. When you're in it, you don't see anything else."

"I know and when she goes back to college, it gets hard for them, though we're letting her take her car this year so she can go back and forth, making it easier on them since he goes to school up here. He's got one more year before he heads to the academy. Unfortunately, right now my daughter's car is in the shop, so dad becomes the uber driver since the boys need their car for work." Jared ran a hand over the top of his head. "I thought it was rough when they were all under the age of ten. But this adult and teenage thing is killing me."

An image of Lisa filled Foster's brain. He wondered what she would have looked like as a teenager. Would her hair have gotten darker like his? Or would it have stayed more of a lighter brown like her mother's? Would she have been tall like him? Or on the shorter side like Victoria?

As if Jared knew what Foster was thinking, he reached out and squeezed his biceps. Jared had been one of the first troopers to respond to the fire the night Lisa died. He stood next to Foster when they pulled Lisa's body from the rubble. After that moment, the entire night became a blur. Foster lost his shit.

Jared had always been kind to him and offered his ear, but Foster never took him up on it. Instead, Foster shut down.

Until recently.

"Do you have a few minutes? I've always wanted to talk to you about something, but never had the chance."

"What about Caitlyn and her boyfriend?" Foster asked.

"I was just going to pick him up to bring him back here. I guess he loaned his vehicle to his little brother or something. Anyway, I can let Caitlyn go get him. It might be good for both of us to have a little space right now."

"I've got a little time."

"Why don't we go have a seat over there." Jared pointed to a table off to the side of the main house near a summer kitchen.

Foster sipped his coffee and strolled down the

path. His cell buzzed in his back pocket. He pulled it out and smiled.

Tonya: *Is my landlord going to lecture you? Haha. Sorry. I glanced out the window while eating toast and saw you talking with Jared.*

Foster: *That's funny. Just having a friendly manly chat. I didn't want to be rude.*

He took a seat and stared at a sailboat floating on the lake. The tall mast swung back and forth in the slight breeze. He should be uncomfortable. He didn't like having any part of his life open for discussion. Being a private man was more important to him than having people in his life.

Somehow that concept had slowly shifted. He'd felt that change deep in his core over the last few years as he developed friendships with Tonya and her family and Doug and Jim, but he still managed to keep his walls up.

Tonya managed to knock it down in an instant and he found himself scrambling to try to rebuild it, only he wasn't sure why.

Except he was utterly terrified of not being able to go the distance and that would destroy her.

"Sometimes I don't understand Caitlyn," Jared said as he pulled out a chair and sat down with a long sigh. "When I told her to take the truck, she was disappointed I wasn't making the drive with her. We're all spending the day together."

"Perhaps she wanted to plead her case again, or maybe to apologize."

"Maybe," Jared said. "When Calvin first started wanting to date her last year, she was just graduating high school, and I wasn't ready for her to fall in love, but that's what was happening right in front of my eyes."

"That has to be hard for you to admit."

"It's getting easier. Ryan keeps telling me she doesn't believe Calvin is going anywhere and that I need to get used to him being part of this family, so that's what I'm doing. It does help that from the moment I met him, I had a good feeling about him and I trust my gut." He leaned forward, resting his hands on the table. "We've known each other for a long time, but we don't know each other well."

Foster couldn't argue that point. "I don't put myself out there."

"I know and I respected your space after the fire because, while my story is so different, I experienced the same loss."

That was information that Foster hadn't heard. Not that he listened to gossip, mostly because he didn't talk to anyone. "What do you mean?"

"A very long time ago, I was married to someone else. It didn't last very long. We got divorced, in part because my ex-wife thought I paid more attention to Ryan, who lived in my carriage house, but there were a million other reasons. She left me to take care of our infant son, Johnny. At the time, I wasn't equipped to be father, much less a single one. When he died, I blamed myself."

"I had no idea." Foster's heart dropped to the pit of his stomach. This was the kind of pain that no matter what anyone did, you just didn't get past it. It lived in the center of your soul for as long as you lived. "I'm so sorry. How did he die?"

"Unknown cause. It happened in his sleep. I was devastated and for a long time, I kept people away, including Ryan. I was even going to sell this house and move across the state. But then a series of events happened and things changed between Ryan and me. I found that all I had been doing was holding on to the pain of what I'd lost, instead of letting it flow through me so I could come out the other side." Jared swiped at his eyes. "Don't get me wrong. When I think of him or allow myself to travel back in time, I live it all again. It's been two decades and the pain still cuts right through my heart." He tapped his chest. Tears welled. "But allowing love back in gave me reason to live my life to the fullest instead of torturing myself as if that was what I deserved. I might be overstepping, which my wife tells me I do all the time; however, when I see you, it's like looking in a mirror."

That was heavy. Deep. And maybe too much this early in the morning. Foster appreciated Jared's heart-felt honesty. Not many people would be so brutal with their truth. A couple of months ago, Foster would have stood, thanked Jared, and left. However, one of the things he was working on in therapy was letting people in, especially those whom he shared a common bond.

He certainly had that with Jared.

"A piece of me died that night," Foster managed. His throat was dry, but his lukewarm coffee didn't suffice.

"I felt the same way. But it's not true. We're both hardened and we both understand how easily our loved ones can be taken from us, which is why I didn't allow anyone in for the longest time. Even when I was falling hard for Ryan, I still continued with my move to Rochester. I told myself she was too young for me. That it was a goodbye thing. That all I was going to do was break her heart because I couldn't give her what she wanted most. A family."

Yeah. That was about right. Foster nodded in agreement. No point in lying to a man who bared his soul.

"Do you want to know what I learned, besides the fact that I'm a stubborn fool?"

Foster laughed. "Sure."

"It wasn't Ryan's heart I was afraid of hurting, but my own." Jared arched a brow. "I held on to my loss like a badge of honor. The way I blamed myself allowed me to push people away so I never had to feel that kind of pain again. I didn't know that's what I was doing until I got in my car and drove away, leaving behind the only woman I ever truly loved. It was that moment I understood what I'd been doing. I believe, if you look closely, you're in the same boat." He glanced over his shoulder. "I'm glad to see you here, but I can see the conflict in your eyes. Take it from this old man, don't fight it. I know that's the first instinct. You tell yourself that it's best to cut and run. Because you're a good man, you don't want to hurt Tonya and I can appreciate that thinking, but at the end of the day, you're not doing either one of you any favors."

Foster blew out a puff of air and leaned back in his chair. He contemplated every single word Jared shared. He took a few moments to gather his thoughts. "I honestly don't know if I can do this and it's not fair to her," he finally admitted. Jared had been real with him, so it was time for Foster to be real with someone else. His therapist would be proud. Two male bonding experiences in one week and a sexual encounter with a woman he truly cared about. It was surreal. "When I'm with Tonya, everything changes. It's been like that for a while, but I've never acted on it. I probably never would have had she not put it out there. I was content with the way my life was. I know I had issues, but I've been working on them."

"Can I ask you a question?"

"Sure."

"What is it about being with Tonya that you don't think you can do?"

"The family part," he said. "I don't want to have another child. Besides being thirty-seven years old—"

"Hey. I was almost thirty-six when I had Caitlyn and forty-one when Bella was born, so the age thing isn't really a thing."

"Did you want more?"

"Not at first," Jared said. "As a matter of fact, I couldn't even hold a baby. When Ryan's brother had a child, and he wanted me to be the godfather, I was mortified and a bit angry. I never wanted to love anyone again. That hurt, but as time went on, I realized I didn't want to live my life without Ryan and once I accepted that, I wanted the world with her and that included a family." He waved his hands toward the house. "Had she not cut me off after we had Bella, I would have a couple more, but I wouldn't change a thing about my life."

"This is not something I tell people, so I'd appreciate it if we kept it between us."

"Everything about this conversation is private."

"Thank you," Foster said. "After Lisa died and Victoria went to jail, I drank myself into oblivion. Not so much out of depression, but more because I wanted to understand the addiction. I also took some pills. I wanted to know what the romance was between Victoria and the drugs. Anyway, I landed myself in a psyche hold. That's where I met my therapist."

"That's a tough place to be and I'm glad you're still kicking."

"Truthfully, so am I," Foster said. "I never wanted to harm myself. I just wanted to know."

"Did you learn anything?"

Foster shook his head. "I still don't understand and I probably never will. However, I've spent a few years talking about why I've shut myself off from life. The idea of starting over is terrifying and I don't want to do it. I've enjoyed existing. There's a fair amount of freedom in it. I don't have to answer to anyone. I'm not responsible to anyone."

"No offense, man, but isn't that lonely at times?"

"I didn't know it was until Tonya opened Pandora's box."

Jared laughed. "Yeah. I remember that feeling." He lifted his leg, resting his ankle on his knee. "Ryan propositioned me when I informed her that I was moving. She wanted a one-night stand. I was floored, but more so, totally tempted and that was an unexpected feeling. I didn't know I thought of her that way. I mean, I saw her as a woman, but she is ten years younger and I've known her since she was two."

"That's got to be weird."

"It was at first, but I got over that real quick," Jared said. "I kept telling her that I was leaving, and she kept saying she was fine with it."

"I've made it clear to Tonya that I can't give her what she wants and yet I found myself here last night and I didn't leave. I don't know what I'm doing, and while I agree with you that I might be afraid of having my heart broken, I will hate myself when I break hers."

"That's a definitive statement."

"It's true," Foster said. "It doesn't matter how much I care about her, or even if I can get past the long-term commitment thing. I'm never going to want children again."

"If I haven't shoved my boot in my mouth yet, I'm going to do it right now." Jared dropped his foot to the patio with a heavy thud. He shifted his chair and stared at Foster intently. "Is it because you feel like you'll be replacing Lisa?"

Foster sucked in a deep breath, but no oxygen filled his lungs. It was as if he flew through the air and landed on his back, having the wind knocked out of him.

"I thought so," Jared said softly, glancing toward the sky. "Johnny was my firstborn. I loved him more than anything. Every year on his birthday, me and my kids go visit his grave. They bring him toys. It breaks my heart they never knew him. It kills me that I never got to watch him grow up or have fights with him over girls or catch him trying to sneak out of the house, like I did the twins last weekend. The little fuckers. I've never once tried to replace Johnny. I can't. Not a day goes by that I don't think about him. I miss him terribly." Jared choked on his last few words. "Shit.

I'm sorry. I really didn't mean to go this deep. I just wanted you to know about my son and that I'm here if you ever wanted to talk."

"I appreciate that."

Jared swiped at his eyes. He'd always been a fair and decent man. Even when in uniform, he showed compassion. Last year, when Lake and Tiki were going through their drama, Jared made sure the press and everyone around them gave the couple space. He bent the rules when necessary. No one could ever describe Jared as someone who tossed his weight as a cop around, although Foster wouldn't want to find himself on the wrong side of the law in his jurisdiction. He'd seen him in action a couple of times, and Jared was badass.

"I kept you long enough and I said way too much," Jared said.

"No. You've given me a lot to think about and not many people understand what I've been through. They try, but it's impossible to wrap your brain around it unless you've lived it."

"No truer words have been spoken." Jared stood, stretching out his arm. "If you ever need anything, consider this a safe space."

Foster took his hand in a firm shake. "Thanks. I'll see you around." He strolled up the path toward his truck, glancing at the carriage house. The conflicted emotions hadn't settled. Jared was right. While his loss was the same, his story was different. Foster could agree that some of his fear was about protecting his own heart and soul.

However, he'd already experienced the worst pain a person could live through. He could endure being hurt by a woman.

What he couldn't live with was causing that kind of pain to another human.

8

"*H*ey, Grandpa." Tonya opened her grandfather's door and stepped into the foyer.

No response.

"Where are you?" They had made plans for lunch a few days ago, but she hadn't talked to him since. Her parents had gone to visit her mom's sister and they had asked her to check in on him, which wasn't a big deal. She loved spending time with him, but it was strange for him not to respond to a text or for him not to call her back. "Grandpa? Hello? I'm here. I've got your favorite sub from Angelo's."

"In the master bathroom," his voice rang out, only it was weak and shaky.

"Are you okay?"

"No."

She dropped the bag and her purse and raced up the stairs and flung open the door.

Her grandfather sat on the toilet, hunched over, wearing a pair of jeans, gripping his elbow. "I fell and I think I broke my arm."

"You scared the crap out of me." For the last year, everyone had been worried about her grandfather living alone, but he was about as stubborn as they came and he refused to move in with her parents. Even Gael and Tayla offered to take him in. Lake and Tiki too.

But her grandpa refused.

Maybe this would be his wake-up call.

"Do you think you can put your shirt on and we can drive to urgent care, or should I call an ambulance?" One thing she'd learned about her grandfather over the years had been to put him in the driver's seat of his life. As long as the choices were appropriate. Either way, he was going to get an X-ray and see a doctor.

"You can drive me."

"When did you fall?" She found his shirt on the floor and helped him put it on. "Did you hit your head?" She did her best to examine him without him noticing while he dressed.

He groaned and cussed like a drunken sailor. Nothing new there. Maxwell Johnson had always had a colorful mouth.

"Maybe ten minutes before you got here." He

stood. "I think there's an arm brace from when I broke my other arm a couple years ago in the closet in the other bathroom."

"Then sit your ass back down while I go get it." Another thing she'd figured out about her grandfather was that she couldn't let him bulldoze her when he needed help. He didn't like to be a burden and the older he got, the more he needed his family instead of the other way around and that frustrated him, which is why she often went to him when she needed guidance. However, he often gave her the best advice.

She rummaged through the closet until she found what she was looking for and made her way back to the master where she found her grandfather sitting on the edge of the bed.

"I can put that on myself." He stood on wobbly legs.

She wasn't about to argue with him. Based on the way he talked, he was fine. Her only concern, outside of the arm, was how her grandfather seemed to be deteriorating right in front of her eyes. Granted, he wasn't a spring chicken and the aging process had certainly caught up to him these last few years. However, something seemed off about him and she wanted him to have a complete physical. This might be the perfect opportunity.

"That's fine, but you're going to let me help you down the stairs, whether you like it or not."

He laughed. "You remind me of your grandmother."

"You tell me that every time you think I grow a backbone." She took him by his good arm and guided him down the stairs. She wanted to give him a good lecture about how he should be living on the lower level. Or how he should move, but she'd save that for after the visit to the doctor.

"You should be this confident all the time. I like the ring in your voice."

Inwardly, she rolled her eyes. Behaving as if she were self-assured in every situation wasn't in her wheelhouse. If she didn't feel as though she knew what she was doing, or had a solid relationship with the people she was dealing with, she tended to be soft-spoken. It took her a while to settle into anything. She believed there was a time and a place and more often than not, it was never the right time for her to flex her voice.

She wasn't like Tayla. Calling her assertive was being kind, although describing her oldest sister as aggressive would be too harsh. Nor was Tonya like Tiki who in her darkest hour took the bull by the horns and turned her life around.

All her life, Tonya had been the quiet sister. The overlooked sister. The sister that sometimes people forgot was in the room.

"Your grandmother retreated inwardly like you

do. I never understood it. I still don't. She was such an incredible woman and so are you." He paused at the bottom of the stairs, gripping his cane with his good arm, and glanced up. "How are things going between the two of you?"

She sighed. She was going to bring this topic up anyway. "It's good, but it's weird." Nudging her grandpa toward the front door, she snagged her purse and the subs that she'd tossed to the floor. Knowing her grandfather, he'd be bitching that he was starving in about a half hour and it might take a while, even at urgent care.

"You're going to have to explain what you mean by that." He grumbled and groaned and swore under his breath while he hobbled out the door. It got worse when he climbed into the passenger seat of her vehicle.

Carefully, she backed out of the driveway and headed toward the main road. As she passed her parents' house, and then Tayla and Gael's, she realized she should have texted them what happened. She'd do that as soon as she got into town. It would only take fifteen or so minutes.

"I'm waiting," her grandpa said.

"Oh. Right. Weird." She gripped the steering wheel. Some might think her relationship with her grandfather was strange, but she cherished it. He could be judgmental about her decisions, but he was never cruel. He always supported her and gave her a shoulder to cry on when she needed it most. "He's running hot and cold."

"Not that I really want to know, but have the two of you—you know." He waved his hand in a mini circle.

Her cheeks flushed.

"Because if you have, that changes everything. I know with your generation it happens much faster than back in my day, but I'm going to assume it still has an impact on the relationship."

"Of course it does and that's why I think he's acting strange. I can't tell if he regrets it. Or is running scared. Or what."

"I can't believe I'm going to say this, but you're going to have to give me more details." He shook his head. "This would be easier if I had boy grand-children."

"Dad told me you sucked at the sex talk when he was a teenager." She laughed. "But without going into too much depth, he was going to leave the other morning without saying goodbye. Then he kept his distance for a little while when I showed up in the kitchen, but something switched and he got friendly. We had a nice moment. However, since then, I've barely talked to him. It feels like he's avoiding me."

"Have you asked him about it?"

"No." She did her best to avoid all the potholes the winter caused as well as not taking the corners too tight. Luckily, there wasn't any traffic and they made it into the village in record time. The new urgent care facility was south of town and she made the light, which was nice.

"Why don't you call him while I'm in the exam room."

She pulled into the parking lot and found a space close to the front door. "Because you're not getting rid of me that easily."

"I'm a grown-ass man."

"Never said you weren't." She shut the engine off. "But you have a tendency these days to be a secret keeper when it comes to your health." She slipped from the car and raced to the passenger side, helping her grandpa into the building. She noticed he'd lost some weight. "If I let you go in alone, you won't tell me what the doctor said."

There wasn't a single person in the waiting room. She helped her grandpa fill out all the forms and the nurse took his vitals and brought him back to get some X-rays, leaving her in the exam room by herself.

Quickly, she shot off a text to her family. Immediately, her cell rang.

"Hey, Dad," she said.

"What the hell happened and why didn't you tell us sooner?"

"I thought it was best to get him to urgent care while he was agreeable. They are taking pictures now. He's being his usual ornery self."

"Something is going on with him," her dad said.

"I know. He's lost a ton of weight. We need to get him in to see his regular doctor and someone needs to go with him."

"I've tried. So has your mother, but that man is as stubborn as a mule when it comes to this shit. Maybe you will have better luck."

"I'll work on it." She heard the shuffling of her grandpa's feet. "I gotta go. I'll text you when we're on our way home."

The technician smiled as she pulled out a chair for her grandfather. "The nurse practitioner will be with you after she reads the images."

"Thank you," Tonya said.

"Based on how much that hurt, I bet it's broken." Her grandpa slumped in the chair. "I know I need to admit defeat and living in that big house alone isn't smart. But I'm not ready to lose my independence."

"Oh, Grandpa. I know this isn't easy." She moved her chair closer, resting a hand on his knee. "But it's time to consider living with Mom and Dad."

A tap at the door startled Tonya. She lifted her gaze.

"Mr. Johnson," a vaguely familiar voice said. "I have some bad news."

"I thought so." Her grandfather sighed.

Tonya swallowed her pulse.

"Oh. You're Foster's friend." Kathy lowered the X-ray image. "I can't remember your name."

"It's Tonya."

"Good to see you again." Kathy lifted the image and clipped it to a film illuminator on the wall. "What's your relationship to my patient?"

"He's my grandfather." Tonya's muscles tensed. "How bad is the break?"

"The good news is that it's a clean one. It doesn't need to be set and we can cast it right here." She tapped her pencil where a line in the bone appeared. "What happened?"

"I lost my balance and fell."

"Does that happen a lot?" Kathy asked.

"It's been happening more and more." Tonya didn't like discussing her grandfather's issues with Kathy, but she was the professional in this situation. "I think he should have a complete physical with his regular doctor."

Her grandfather raised his hand. "I'll make sure that happens. Now, can we please cast this arm? It hurts like hell."

"Sure. I'll send in the tech. If you don't have an orthopedic doctor, I can recommend one because you'll need to follow up in three weeks."

"I know a guy," her grandfather said. "But thanks."

"Not a problem." Kathy turned and curled her fingers over the door handle. She paused and glanced over her shoulder. "Please tell Foster to call me. I've left him a couple of messages. It's important." She disappeared down the hallway.

"How does she know Foster?" Her grandpa arched a brow.

"It doesn't matter and we're not telling him we saw her. She's not important."

9

*T*onya understood that Foster was busy. It was wedding season and they both were under the gun in so many ways, but the last two times they spoke, he brushed her off.

She glanced at her watch.

He was late. Only fifteen minutes, but still. He'd promised he would join her for dinner with Gael and Tayla.

A double date.

Only, it shouldn't feel too weird for him since it wasn't like the four of them hadn't been together before.

The waitress arrived with a bottle of red. She opened it and let Gael smell and taste before pouring three glasses, leaving the fourth empty.

Tonya dug into her purse and pulled out her cell.

No texts.

She checked her last message, making sure she'd given him the right restaurant and time.

He'd responded with a thumbs-up about two hours ago. That was a typical response. However, things had changed, and his messages back to her should have too, so it would have been nice to have something a little more intimate and personal.

Tayla leaned forward and grabbed her hand. "What's going on with you?"

Dropping her phone back into her pocketbook, she sighed. No reason to lie to her sister. "Foster is acting weird ever since he spent the night."

"You and he slept together?" Tayla asked with a high-pitched voice. "When did that happen? Why are you just telling me this now? And what do you mean by weird, exactly? I can't believe you've been holding out on me."

"This isn't our business," Gael said. "But now that the cat is out of the bag, I'd like to know the answers too."

"The only thing I'm going to say about it is that I feel like he's avoiding spending any amount of time with me. Like he might regret it or something." Tonya held back the gut-wrenching emotion that filled her heart. Foster had warned her that he wasn't sure about his ability to do a relationship. Or that he could go the distance. So had her grandfather. She'd gone into this with the idea that life came with risks. That being passive was no way to live.

But she didn't think she'd find out so quickly that Foster would cut and run.

"Have you talked to him about it?" Gael asked.

"We've barely spent any real time together this week. I stopped by the worksite and brought him lunch. That was nice, but it was twenty minutes before something happened and he had to go. And he acted distant. I don't want to come off as needy and scare him away, but I might have already done that."

"We don't have to stay." Tayla smiled sweetly. "We can come up with some work emergency that needs our attention."

"That would be awkward. Besides, who knows if he's even coming now." It wouldn't be the first time that Foster stood her up, only in the past, they hadn't been bed partners. He always had a reason. It usually had something to do with Victoria. Sometimes it would be because he couldn't find her and he wanted to continue the search. Or it would be she was in a bad way and he wanted to check on her, making sure she had food and water. Other times it was because she was drying out and he had some hope she would get clean and sober.

Of course, there were times that Foster just went dark. She'd gotten used to all these idiosyncrasies about the elusive man, but that had been before they'd become intimate. Before he'd told her he cared about her as if she could be his girlfriend.

Now that she'd had a taste, she wanted more and

she knew he might not be capable. That was something she was going to have to live with. She just hadn't expected it would end as abruptly as it began.

"He's here," Gael said.

Tonya sucked in a deep breath and let it out slowly. She glanced over her shoulder, wishing she hadn't.

He waved, smiling that dashing grin as he strolled across the main floor of the restaurant. "So sorry I'm late." He leaned in and kissed her cheek, giving her shoulder a good squeeze.

The physical contact should make her feel better.

But for some reason, it didn't. Instead, it only served to grate on her nerves, making her want to take him aside and either end it or get past whatever the hell was going on in his mind.

He shook Gael's hand before sitting down. "The owners of the Mason project showed up on-site today and had Doug and Jim going over every detail. They asked if I could stay. It was really cool to see them in action. It was a bit intimidating, but I also learned a lot."

"No worries. We're just glad you could make it." Gael reached across the table and poured Foster a glass of wine. "How long have you worked for Sutter and Tanner Construction?"

"I started very part-time five years ago, but these past two years they've brought me on full-time for certain projects and I'm thinking I might want to make it a career. They are willing to let me work around my wedding driver gig," Foster said. "It's a far cry from my family business and a high-pressure sales job, but I really like it."

Gael laughed. "I never thought I'd go from Wall Street to fashion, but look at me now."

"You are far from a fashionista, my love." Tayla patted Gael's shoulder. "While he has good taste in clothing, he doesn't understand the first thing about fabrics or what goes well together. But he gets an *A* for effort."

"You'd be lost without me, darling." Gael winked.

"That is true." Tayla laughed. "But not when it comes to the sewing room."

Tonya loved seeing her sister so happy. Gael had come into her life when her career was ripping at the seams. He helped her see what was truly important. He gave her the ability to follow her dreams without compromising her goals and destroying her relationships with her family.

He was truly a knight in shining armor.

"I'm glad my days of needing to be dressed up are over," Foster said. "Even on wedding boat ride days, it's jeans and a nice button-down shirt."

"Speaking of which, I have some shirts I want to give you," Tayla said. "From my new line. If you don't mind being a walking advertisement for me."

"Not at all, considering you have a sign for my business in your store." Foster lifted his glass and took a sip. "So, did I miss any interesting conversation?" He rested his arm around the back of the booth, his fingers toying with the strands of her long hair.

Tonya found it strange that he seemed so at ease considering the last time she saw him it felt like he couldn't wait to get away. He hadn't kissed her hello— or goodbye. Just a squeeze of the biceps, which felt cold and barely caring for someone whom she thought of as her boyfriend.

She didn't believe that label was too much to ask after allowing him into her bed.

"We'd been wondering how Tiki and Lake were doing on their honeymoon and if they have been able to put work away." Kudos to Gael for jumping back into the beginning of their discussions.

"Knowing them, I doubt it," Foster said. "Work is relaxing to them, which I can relate to. I never thought manual labor would be so fun."

"I can almost relate." Gael shook his head, laughing.

Foster shrugged. "It helps clear the mind and gives me all the physical workout I need. And it's giving me some ideas for what I want to do to my place."

Tonya let out a laugh. She covered her mouth. "Sorry. It's just that you've been saying you're going to fix that place up for as long as I've known you. All you've done is build the loft for your bedroom and fix up the boathouse." She held up her hand when he opened his mouth. "Which, by the way, all look amazing; it's just that you constantly talk about different things you could do. One day it's expanding. Next day it's—"

He pressed his finger over her lips. "I asked Doug to draw up plans today to put on an addition, clear out the waterfront, take out all those trees and brush that make you crazy because you don't think I let in enough sunlight."

"Are you serious? You're actually going to let Doug and Jim renovate?"

"I'm letting them do the plans. We'll go from there." He rested his hand on the back of her neck and massaged gently. "They get focused on the value of the property and sometimes that bothers me. I can't imagine selling it. Or renting it, but they think I could get more than twice what I paid for it."

Mixed messages.

Her grandfather told her that would happen with a man like Foster. After his arm had been casted, he told her, like he needed to make changes in his life-style, she needed to be more assertive in her wants and needs. It was time to tell Foster what her true expectations were.

"Well, well, well," a familiar female voice grated against her ears. "Twice in one week. It must be fate."

Tonya twisted in the booth and made eye contact with Kathy. Inwardly, she groaned.

It was actually three times for her, not that she was counting. Her heart dropped. She'd never told Foster she'd seen Kathy. When they talked about her grandfather and his broken arm, it wasn't about where they had gone, but the treatment and game plan going forward. And frankly, the conversation had been rushed.

Kathy planted one hand on her hip and smiled, only she didn't look overly happy. "Hello, Foster. Tonya." She pointed at Tayla. "Do I know you?"

"This is my sister, Tayla. She owns the boutique down the street—"

"Oh, yes. I've window-shopped there. Weren't you a designer in New York or something?" Kathy asked.

What a freaking bitch. Tonya generally didn't have a mean bone in her body, but this woman grated on her last nerve.

"I'm still a designer," Tayla said with a beaming smile and pride laced to her words. "I hope you'll come check out my store sometime."

"Perhaps." Kathy smacked her lips. "So, Foster. We keep running into each other. That has to mean something."

"All it means is that I've started getting out more. Now if you don't mind, we're in the middle of having a nice dinner before you interrupted." Foster fiddled with his wineglass, not glancing up.

"Hmm. I take it Tonya didn't give you my message," Kathy said.

He shifted his gaze, giving Tonya a sideways glance.

"No. I didn't." Tonya squared her shoulders.

"That was rude." Kathy sighed and shook her head. "You had no business not telling him."

"This isn't the time or place," Foster said under his breath. "I think it's time for you to go."

"Fine. But we do need to talk. I'll be in touch." Kathy turned on her heel and marched off.

Foster downed half his beverage. "I need to get some fresh air. Will you please excuse me?" He didn't wait for anyone to respond. He stood, filled his glass, and stormed out the side door toward the docks attached to the restaurant.

"What was that all about?" Tayla asked.

"Not my story to tell." Tonya lifted her napkin off her lap and placed it on the table. However, she wasn't about to let Foster's mood fester very long. He'd been avoiding her and now Kathy ruined what had started to be a nice night.

Something had to give.

It was time to lay her cards on the table and find out if this relationship was going somewhere or if it was time to call it quits.

Foster stepped out into the evening air. He'd avoided Kathy for years, and seeing her again only reminded him why he'd tortured himself since Lisa had died. After his conversation with Jared, he knew he had some serious soul-searching to do, and he'd come to the conclusion that he owed it to himself, his daughter, and Tonya to give life a chance.

Then Kathy had to walk into the restaurant and twist his gut. He shouldn't be mad at Tonya for not telling her who took care of Maxwell. The fact of the matter was he should have known the moment Tonya had mentioned they had gone to urgent care.

"Foster," Tonya said with a stern tone. "Wait up."

He paused in the middle of the dock, staring out at the lake. Country music filled the air. A few other couples strolled down the wood planks, holding hands and enjoying the romantic ambiance. He turned and leaned against one of the pylons. "I'm sorry. I shouldn't have let her get to me again, but she really has a way of getting under my skin. She can be relent-less and I tried being nice. I can't go through this with her again, and I feel bad that you and your family are now in the middle of it."

"I probably should have told you that I ran into her, but you haven't made it easy for me to have a conversation with you lately."

"This week was busy."

"I'll give you that." She stood a few feet away. "However, now that we've been together, you're acting like you don't want to be around me."

He opened his mouth, but she held up her hand.

"I knew when I asked you out that things could go sideways. I know what you've been through and what you think you're capable of and I respect that. I'm a big girl and if this is where this is going to end, then I'm okay with that. Actually, I'd rather do it now, before we end up hating each other. Your friendship is more important to me."

He set his drink on the post. "I suck at relationships." He ran a hand across the top of his head. "I don't want things to end, and I'm sorry that I avoided you."

"So I wasn't crazy."

"But it's not what you think." He reached out and cupped the side of her face. "We went a little too fast and I needed some time to think. To slow down. I wanted to talk to you about it. However, it was never the right time, or I didn't know what to say."

"Yeah. You should have said something."

"I know." He brushed his mouth over her sweet lips. "I wish you would have told me about Kathy, though."

"It's been seven years. She's a smart woman. Why is she holding on to you?"

"She told me that someday I'd come back to her and I told her that would never happen. At the courthouse, after Victoria's sentencing, I said some of the most horrible things I could have ever said to someone."

"Like what?"

He turned, planting his hands on his hips. If he was going to seriously give this relationship a go,

JEN TALTY

Tonya had the right to know the truth. Well, some of it. At least his version of it. "I started by telling her that she meant nothing to me. That she never did and that if there had been a way to send her to prison with my ex-wife, I would have because that night I had planned on leaving earlier. Kathy liked hiding my keys. It was a stupid, childish game she played with me and we ended up—well, it doesn't matter. I'm a grown man who made a bad decision. I told Kathy she might as well have set the house on fire with Victoria and that I wished she could trade places with Lisa."

"Jesus, Foster. That's cruel."

He sighed. "Does it help that I apologized for it later?"

"Perhaps a little." She came up behind him, wrapping her arms around his waist and resting her head on his back.

"I was angry at the world. She didn't deserve those words and I do regret saying them. However, she spent the next few months harassing me. She called me or texted me every day. She'd show up at my house. I had to threaten her and she finally went away. Mostly. I mean, she has reached out every once in a while, but I ignore her."

"So what changed? Why is she all of a sudden in hot pursuit?"

He turned, holding Tonya close, staring into her kind, warm eyes. "I'm guessing it was seeing you and

136

me together. The idea that I moved on and am dating someone that isn't her doesn't settle well."

"Oh. I hadn't thought about that."

"It's the only thing I can think of." He kissed her nose. "I don't mean to be so moody. I'll work on being a better boyfriend."

She tilted her head. "Did you just say boyfriend?"

"Too weird?"

"No. I like the sound of it." She raised up on tiptoe and kissed him, hard. It was the kind of kiss that shouldn't be done in a public place.

Normally, he hated all public displays of affection. But not tonight. He wrapped his arms tightly around her waist and heaved her to his chest. His tongue swirled around hers in a hot, wild dance. His body wanted to forget about dinner and go straight back to his place, but that would be rude. Reluctantly, he pulled back. "We should get back to your sister and her husband." He took her by the hand and guided her toward the newly renovated restaurant that had been closed down for two years. "I've been looking forward to checking out this place. Did you know that Doug and Jim did the work?"

"I remember you helping them." Tonya laughed. "You told me that three ex-military brothers own the Blue Moon."

"I think they were special forces. Quiet types," he said. "I met them the other day. Nice men. Lake's sister seemed to be interested in one of them."

"Quiet describes you." She nudged him with her hip. "There are times when hanging with you the silence is deafening."

"I'm working on that." He opened the door off the patio and did his best not to let his mood sour again as they passed Kathy's table.

She sat with three other girlfriends, one of which he recognized. It didn't matter. That was his past.

Tonya was his future.

10

"Hey." Tonya squeezed Foster's shoulder as they approached his truck in the parking lot after saying goodbye to her sister and Gael. "We can go look for Victoria before we head home."

"I'm sorry. I didn't mean to put a damper on such a wonderful evening."

"You didn't." Being with Foster meant that Victoria was part of their relationship. Tonya accepted that long before she asked him out. She didn't pretend to understand his attachment to his ex-wife, but she'd support it.

"Last time I saw her, she was hanging in the alley across the street, but my sources told me she's been sick or something."

"What kind of sick?"

"A friend of hers said she's been limping. Maybe

injured. But she hasn't been around much and he's been worried."

She'd been with him on numerous occasions where they'd searched for hours, chatting with various men and women living on the streets. They had a code they lived by, and most wouldn't break it. However, they did care deeply for one another, for the most part, and when one was hurting, they would often tell a trusted outsider.

Foster didn't always fit that bill. Some of Victoria's friends stayed clear of Foster because he'd broken Victoria's trust a time or two. They viewed him as someone who would call the cops or turn them in. But they had no problem taking his food. However, there were a few who believed Foster cared and they would always give him good information.

"Did he have specifics?" she asked.

"Not really. But why don't we walk, and on the way back, we can get an ice cream, if you want."

"That sounds nice."

In silence, they made their way toward the convenience store, where they stopped and picked up a few things for Victoria and others. The alley was two more side streets away. It wasn't the best part of town, but it wasn't unsafe either. It amazed her how many homeless people there were in the village. It broke her heart, but at the same time, it made her feel as though she was a bad person for not doing enough to help them.

He handed out water and bags of chips. Everyone smiled and thanked Foster, many using his name. Two people pointed down the alley, indicating Victoria's location. "There she is," Foster said, holding Tonya's hand harder.

It was never easy for him to see Victoria this way. He had a big heart and even though he still placed blame on her for what happened, he wanted her to get help.

"Victoria," he said calmly.

She sat against the building, her legs stretched out, dirt covering her ratty, ripped jeans. She had no shoes and her feet had dried blood on them. She wiped her long, greasy hair from her face. "Did you bring me money?"

"No." He knelt down. "I've got food and water." He set the bag next to her and tentatively ran a hand over her ankle. "It looks like you were bleeding. Did you get hurt?"

"I'm fine. I need money."

"Maybe we should go get you checked out." He reached out and tilted her chin. A cut appeared on the side of her face, along with a nasty bruise. "What happened here?"

"I'm not your concern anymore." She opened the bag. "Thanks for the food. Can I have some money?"

"You know I'm not giving you cash because you'll spend it on drugs."

"I could sell this for the same thing."

Tonya noticed a large tear in her left thigh. She bent over and got a closer look. It wasn't good. Puss oozed out of the wound. She tugged at Foster's sleeve. "We need to take her to the hospital," she whispered.

"Why?"

"Her leg's infected." She pointed.

Foster pressed the back of his hand on Victoria's cheek. "You're burning up."

"It's hot out," Victoria said.

"It's seventy-five degrees." Foster straightened, taking Tonya by the arm. "She hates hospitals and she doesn't like it when I tell her what to do, especially when she's been drinking."

"She does smell like she bathed in a vat of bourbon."

"That's putting it mildly," Foster said. "I have to tread lightly because she can become belligerent and violent toward me."

"Why don't you let me try to talk to her?"

"I don't want you in the middle and I don't want you getting hurt."

She curled her fingers around his biceps. "She needs medical attention. You're right here. If she even raises her voice, you can step in."

"All right. Thanks."

Tonya blew out a puff of air and collected her thoughts. "Hi, Victoria. I don't know if you remember me or not. I'm Tonya. I'm a friend of Foster's."

"I know who you are." Victoria lifted her gaze. She struggled to twist off the cap of one of the water bottles Foster had bought. "You're the chick who follows him around like a pathetic street cat."

Tonya took the plastic bottle and opened it, ignoring the dis. "Does your leg hurt?"

"It's more numb now, but it hurts if I try to stand," Victoria admitted.

"You have a nasty infection and you need antibiotics. Will you let us take you to the hospital?"

"Does he have to come?"

Tonya glanced over her shoulder. "I know he'd like to, and looking at the cut on your leg, we might need his help."

"Okay." Victoria chugged. "I like your purse. Can I have it?"

"Foster. Give me a hand." She ignored the request.

"Wow. You're going to have to tell me how you got her to agree to go so quickly," he whispered as he hoisted Victoria into his arms.

"Tony, watch all my stuff, okay?" Victoria asked the guy curled up on a mattress across from her things. "I'll be back soon. I got some business to take care of." Her words were slurred.

"You got it, sister." The man waved a hand.

Tonya walked in silence all the way back to Foster's truck. She climbed into the back seat with Victoria, who laid her head in Tonya's lap. A million things raced through Tonya's mind. One was how frail Victoria looked compared to the last time she'd seen the woman. Her skin was wrinkled and hung loose off her bones. She looked twenty years older than she was and the whites of her eyes were yellow. In some ways, it was a miracle she was still alive.

In other ways, it was a shame she still had to suffer.

"When she's sober, she's going to flip out." Foster glanced in the rearview mirror. "Because she won't remember agreeing to this. But worse, she'll start going into withdrawal and that's always a nightmare."

"Let's deal with one thing at a time." Tonya sighed. She'd seen Victoria when she'd gone after Foster once before. In a drug-induced stupor, she agreed to go to rehab. When she sobered up, she came at him with both barrels loaded. Not only did she take a few swings at him, but she cut him with her words. "We're doing the right thing. Her leg is so badly infected that it could cause all sorts of problems if it gets into her bloodstream. It could kill her."

"You know she's trying to do that, right? She just won't do it the easy way." Foster pulled up to the ER entrance. He glanced over his shoulder. "I don't want this for her; I just don't know how much more I can take."

The pain emulating from his sweet, sensitive eyes nearly destroyed Tonya. She understood he felt a sense of responsibility for his ex-wife. She couldn't fault him for it, but she wished he could let some of it go.

An attendant came out to the vehicle. "What's the problem?"

"I've got a homeless woman, age thirty-six, who has a nasty cut on her leg that we believe is infected along with a bruise on her face. I think she has a fever. She's been drinking and is probably on something, but we don't know what. There could be other things wrong," Foster said.

"No insurance, I take it?" the attendant asked.

"I'll take care of the bill," Foster said.

"Okay. Let me get a wheelchair and a parking pass."

"Why don't I park the truck and you go in with Victoria." Tonya slipped from the back seat. "She's out cold."

"Okay. Thanks." He stepped onto the pavement and took her into his arms. "I'm sorry tonight ended this way." He pressed his lips on her forehead. "I'll make it up to you."

"Right now, Victoria is what matters."

"Anyone ever tell you that you're an amazing woman?"

"You just did."

Foster leaned against the wall in the hallway of the hospital, listening to Victoria cuss out the nurse. He pinched the bridge of his nose. It had been three hours since he brought Victoria in and she was finally coming down from whatever she'd been on and the only thing she wanted was a prescription for pain pills.

Which no doctor in their right mind was going to give her, although they did want to admit her, but Foster figured she was going to rip out the IV and leave against medical advice.

It wouldn't be the first time.

The sound of heels clicking against the ugly tile floor caught his attention. He turned his head.

In all of this, Tonya had been a rock. She'd been calm and kind when he wanted to raise the fucking roof. He was tired of being nice. Tired of picking up the pieces. He didn't want to care anymore.

However, he'd made a promise to his daughter the night she'd found her mother passed out on the bathroom floor in her own vomit that he'd always protect her. He hated that Lisa had to see her mom in that state. That's when he had pushed hard to get Victoria into rehab and that was the best few months he and his family had ever experienced.

Until Victoria fell off the wagon and everything went to shit again.

Seven months later, Lisa was dead.

Tonya handed him a cup of coffee that smelled like tar.

He took a sip, and it tasted worse.

"It doesn't sound like it's going too well in there." Tonya gave him a weak smile.

"She's ten minutes away from walking out the door. As soon as the doctor gives her a prescription for antibiotics, she'll leave. If I don't bring her back to the alley, she'll walk, hitch a ride, or whatever."

Tonya rubbed her hand up and down his biceps. "We did the right thing, no matter what she does from this point."

Deep down, he knew she was right.

The curtain opened and out stepped the doctor. "So, she's going to leave and I can't talk her into staying, even though we'd like to treat her with intravenous antibiotics, IV fluids, and run some other tests. I don't believe that infection is contained, and her leaving could be the beginning of the end. I don't believe her liver is functioning properly. I'm not sure about her kidneys, and I won't know until I have the chance to run tests, but she's adamant that's not going to happen."

"I told you." Foster pushed from the wall. "Do I need to stop at a drugstore to fill a prescription?"

"Nope, but she shouldn't drink while she's on the antibiotic. However, she's going to have serious withdrawal if she doesn't. If I know she's staying with you, I can give her something to help." The doctor handed Foster a piece of paper. "She really should come back in five to ten days."

"I'll try, but I wouldn't be surprised if she finds a new alley to sleep in or even heads down to Saratoga just to avoid me."

"She won't be getting along too well on that leg for a while. She wouldn't tell me how it happened. Did she tell either of you?"

"No." Foster shook his head.

"We're lucky she agreed to come here in the first place," Tonya added.

"Any chance you could talk her into a shelter or something?"

"I've got a crazy idea." Tonya took his hand. "Do you think you could get her to stay in the cabin for a couple of days?"

"She's not going to listen to me. We have a deep history and there's a lot of anger there. You know that."

"Why don't you let me try." Tonya arched a brow.

"You're not going in there alone. Not when she's going through withdrawal. She could snap and hurt you."

"If you can get her to stay with you, I'll get you a prescription that will ease her withdrawal symptoms, but we'll have to monitor her, which means I need her back here."

"Let's go." Tonya didn't give him a chance to protest more. She stepped into the exam room.

He groaned. When Tonya finally made up her mind about something, there was no keeping her down. She could be a passionate woman with a big heart. This situation was no exception, only she really didn't know what she was getting into. He stood off the side, but was totally prepared to intervene.

"I can't believe you did this to me." Victoria sat on the edge of the bed and glared. "If the doctor hadn't given me something for my *symptoms* and stitched me up nice, I would have been gone an hour ago."

"Wow. The doctor really did a great job with those." Tonya pointed to Victoria's leg. "But what's going to suck is having to return to get them out. When my older sister got stitches, I took them out for her instead of making the trip back. Why don't you come stay at Foster's cabin so I can do the same for you."

"Why the hell would I do that? I don't want or need his help." Victoria narrowed her stare.

"Oh. I know." Tonya nodded. "But it will save you a trip back here in a week. Plus, I've taken the antibiotics you're going to be on and you really need to eat regularly or it's going to rip your stomach to shreds. I took them once on an empty stomach and was vomiting all day. I'm sure you don't want that. Not to mention the doctor said he'd give us something to help manage the pain and mood swings."

"Well, I don't want to be sick." Victoria let out a long breath.

For the first time in a long time, Foster saw all the

fight leave Victoria's body. Her anger toward him evaporated into thin air.

"Maybe I should stay here overnight like the doctor said." Victoria leaned back and fluffed the pillow. "Would that be too much?"

"Not at all." Foster stepped closer to the edge of the bed. Part of him wanted to reach out and take Victoria's hand. However, he couldn't bring himself to do it. At the base level, he cared for Victoria. He didn't want her to suffer. He certainly didn't want her to die. Not like this.

But forgiveness hadn't come to his heart. Not completely. He had been trying for years. He just couldn't bring himself to do it.

"It's going to cost a small fortune the longer I stay here." Victoria dropped her head back and closed her eyes.

"Let me worry about that," Foster said. "We'll go let the doctor know."

"I should stay," Tonya whispered.

He took Tonya by the hand. For a hot second, he thought about leaving Tonya with Victoria. She could still bolt. He wouldn't put it past her. But he couldn't leave Tonya alone with her either. Tonya wasn't equipped to deal with Victoria and her wicked tongue or vicious temper. "No," he said firmly, tugging her out into the hallway.

"Why did you do that?"

"You don't know her like I do." He leaned against

the wall and folded his arms. "We'll wait here so she can't leave, but you are not staying in there alone."

"And what happens when you need to go to work? I could be alone at your house."

"Nope. I will let Doug and Jim know I'm taking time off and I'll find someone to cover the wedding boat."

Tonya tilted her head.

The curtain slid open.

"What the hell are you doing, Victoria?" Foster shook his head. He had a bad feeling the moment she asked to spend the night. He knew it was too good to be true.

"Fuck you, Foster." Victoria hobbled past him. "As if I'd stay another second in this hellhole. You manipulated me into coming here, and then you got your girlfriend in on it. I'm not staying. I'm certainly not going to stay at your place so you and your little friend can play house. So get out of my way."

"At least wait for the antibiotics," Tonya said. "You need them."

"I'm not your problem and I'm leaving." Victoria smirked.

"I'll drive you," Foster said.

"No. You won't. I made a call to a friend while I was in there. Someone who actually understands me. They are meeting me at the front of the hospital." Victoria limped a few more steps down the hallway.

"Your dealer, I suspect," Foster mumbled.

"I'm not even going to respond." Victoria kept walking.

"Are you just going to let her go?" Tonya asked.

"Yes." Foster had learned a long time ago that there was only so much he could do. His therapist's voice tickled his brain.

You're not her keeper. It's not your responsibility to keep her alive. You have to move beyond the past, live in the present, and think about the future.

He'd taken the horse to water, but she refused to drink.

"Wait," the doctor called. "Here's the antibiotic prescription. You should take this with food."

"I'll make sure she has food every day." Foster glared at Victoria. "Let me give you a ride back to the village."

"Victoria," the doctor said. "If you come back here every day, I can give you something for the withdrawal. You shouldn't drink while you're on this medication. It's not as effective. I also need you to keep that wound clean. If your fever doesn't break or you don't feel better in forty-eight hours, you must come back. This is no joke. You're not in good shape. Do you understand me?"

Victoria nodded. "I don't have any way of getting—"

"Foster and I will make sure you get here," Tonya added.

"If I show up, I show up. Now let's go. I got valuable stuff that we left behind." Victoria refused the hand that Foster offered.

He wasn't about to argue. Instead, he reached for Tonya's. It felt natural. They fit together, making his heart come alive like it hadn't in years. Actually, he wasn't sure he'd ever experienced emotions this intense. This real. Part of him was terrified because while he always wanted Tonya in his life, it had been in the friend zone. He enjoyed her company. She made him laugh and if he needed an ear, she was there.

The intensity of how things changed had scared him and at first he needed time to process. He thought he knew where to take things, but seeing Victoria again showed him that he could never make Tonya happy and it was time to have the difficult conversation.

---

11

*T*onya stared out the window as Foster pulled into the driveway next to the carriage house.

"I'm sorry the evening went sideways. Twice," Foster said.

She chuckled. "I shouldn't laugh. It wasn't funny; it's just how you said it."

"My therapist constantly tells me that I need to lighten up about all this and have a better sense of humor." He put the truck in park and shifted, catching her gaze. "She also tells me I need to find a way to let go."

"I know it's hard."

He glanced at his watch. "It's late and we're both exhausted, but is it okay if I come in?"

"I was hoping you'd spend the night."

He let out a long sigh. "We need to talk."

"I don't like the sound of that. I think I need a drink." She slipped from the cab of the truck and strolled across the path. She tapped the keypad and unlocked the door, Foster one step behind. "Can I get you one?"

"If you've got bourbon, that would be great."

"Sounds like this is a serious chat." She pulled down a glass and handed him a bottle of whiskey while she poured herself a tall glass of red wine and made herself comfortable on the sofa. "You're a good man for doing all you do for Victoria. However, I don't think she will be in that alleyway in the morning." Instead of letting him discuss whatever was on his mind, she decided on the art of deflection. "I'm not a doctor, but that infection was the worst thing I've ever seen."

"That's probably not even the worst of her problems." Foster lifted the drink to his lips and downed half of it before setting it on the coffee table. "She's going to disappear and I feel like it will be my fault."

"No." She placed her hand on his thigh and squeezed. Anything to feel close to him, because she could feel him slipping away.

"When she finally reappears, she'll tell me she left because of me. It's always about something I did."

"You're her scapegoat. You're a convenient way for her not to take responsibility for her life. She's been guilt-tripping you for years." Tonya had never voiced her real feelings about Victoria before. She didn't feel it was her place. She still didn't. However, he brought it up and she felt as though she had nothing to lose. She'd put her heart on the line when it came to Foster. He knew how she felt; whatever happened now was out of her control. There was no reason for her to be anything other than honest with him, about everything.

"You sound like my therapist," he said.

"This isn't any of my business, but I never knew you saw one."

He lifted his arm and rested it on the back of the couch. "It's not something you drop in casual conversation."

"How long have you been going?"

"Shortly after Victoria went to jail, I struggled with wanting to understand addiction and how anyone could put a substance before their family. It didn't work out so well. Ever since then, I've tried to work through my grief. It's been a long, slow process."

"Everyone deals with loss differently." Her mind immediately went to her father and her grandfather. The death of her uncle put a darkness in both their souls. There were so many things that made them sad. Or brought them back to that time and place. They never got over that pain, but they had learned to live through it in a way that it didn't affect their relationships or the quality of their lives. It wasn't easy and there were moments when the tears came hot and fast.

Her father often had to get up, walk away, and collect himself. Sometimes it wasn't any one thing that set him off. The blue sky could remind him of his brother, the love he had for him, and all the memories they didn't have the opportunity to share.

"Did you know that Jared was married before Ryan and that he lost a son?"

"I did," Tonya said. "He doesn't talk much about it. However, he and my grandpa bonded at the cemetery since my uncle is buried a few plots away. There have been times when Jared has picked up my grandfather and taken him so they can sit there and chat, father to father."

Foster laced his fingers through hers and rubbed his thumb over the back of her hand. The gesture surprised her, considering what she thought was coming. "That's really sweet."

"Jared's a good man. A little complicated. Definitely way too old-fashioned for a man not quite sixty."

"I wonder when he's going to retire," Foster said. "He's not that old. His youngest is what? Fifteen? But I don't think he has to work and his job can be dangerous. That has to be hard on his wife and kids."

Tonya sipped her wine. She stretched out her legs and stared at the ceiling. "It's the only life they've ever known. Besides, Jared spends more time managing people than he does on patrol, with the exception of summers. He does like to be out on the water, so he does give himself some shifts there. You'd think there would be some animosity with those who have worked for him forever, wanting to move up the ranks, but there isn't. And there is very little turnover. Stacey, Frank, and Tristen have all been with him forever. Those who have left are no longer state troopers, but still live in the area, like Jake and Josh. They just do other things."

"Jake's the one who owns the horse farm, right?"

"That's right. And Josh's wife—you've met her—is an author with Lake's publishing house. He retired after being shot a few years ago and now works as a PI for Katie and Jackson."

"Still dangerous, especially when you have kids," Foster said.

Tonya shifted her gaze. "You seem to be hooked on the kid and a job that has risks."

He took her chin with this thumb and forefinger. "Things have moved quickly with us. Maybe too quickly."

"We talked about this earlier. I thought we were good. Why did seeing Victoria change things?" The fact that Tonya even voiced her thoughts surprised her because she'd let them fester in her gut in the past. She knew he wanted to give their relationship a real shot; however, there was something in his head—or his heart—that prevented him from giving his whole soul and it was all connected to his past. "You told me that you had feelings for me long before this started.

I'm struggling to comprehend why you keep pulling away every time something emotional happens."

"It's not so much that as I'm constantly reminded of one thing." He dropped his hand to his lap. "I do really care for you. For the last year or so, I've tried not to. I've kept you in the friend zone because you mean a lot to me. But also, I don't want to have more children and I know that's something that's important to you."

She opened her mouth to say something, but he pressed his finger over her lips. "My conversation with Jared had me doing a lot of soul-searching this week and I thought maybe I could move forward with us. That maybe as time passed I would change my mind or you'd be okay with not having children. But that's not fair to either of us, especially when I know this is a deal breaker on both sides."

Tears welled in her eyes. He was right. Living her life without a child wasn't something she thought she could do. She'd always wanted to have kids. There were couples who couldn't have children, but that wasn't by choice. They tried to have them, did everything in their power, but it wasn't in the cards.

This wasn't that.

He was making a conscious decision and now she had to decide if she could live with that.

She dropped her feet to the floor and stood. Making her way toward the kitchen, she set her wine-glass on the counter and pressed her hands on the quartz top. She sucked in a deep breath, letting it out slowly. The night's events swam in her brain like sharks preparing to attack. "I want to understand why you don't want more children." She hadn't met Foster until after the fire, so she hadn't seen him with his daughter. However, she'd heard stories from others about what a great dad he'd been. How devoted he'd been to his darling Lisa.

"I worry that every time I look at that child, I'll resent them because they aren't Lisa."

She squeezed her eyes shut. That was a statement that broke her heart into a million pieces.

"I'm not saying that to hurt you." He came up behind her and rested his hand on the center of her back.

She shrugged it off. She shouldn't have, but right now, she didn't want to be touched by anyone. "You didn't hurt me," she whispered. "I just realized how selfish I've been."

"No. Tonya, you haven't been at all." He took her by the shoulders, forcing her to face him. "All you did was go for what you wanted. That's amazing. You should always do that. I was selfish, thinking this would work itself out, but it won't. I wish I could be the man who gave you everything you need and desire. However, my pain runs too deep and having been in therapy for as long as I have, I know I will never get past it."

Staring into his soft, sweet, blue eyes, she could see

how much he cared for her and walking away from him romantically would be difficult. Learning to be friends with him might prove to be one of the hardest things she'd ever done; however, she would force herself to grow from this experience.

Live and learn.

She put her heart on the line. She loved deeply. And as her grandfather always told her, if you loved once, you could love again. Tiki proved that. And Tonya had other friends who'd been in love, had their hearts crushed, and found even more amazing partners.

She raised up on tiptoe and kissed his cheek. "No regrets and let's make sure we remain friends."

He smiled. "I want that." He squeezed her shoulders. "We have a wedding tomorrow. We can start working on our friendship then."

Swallowing her pride, she walked past him and opened the door. "Drive home safely."

As soon as he stepped through the door, she closed it, locked it, and dropped to the floor, covering her face, letting the hot tears flow freely. But she meant what she said. They had been boyfriend and girlfriend for less than a week and friends for years. The latter was so much more important than a broken heart that would mend.

12

*F*oster spent the next few days looking for Victoria and trying to get Tonya out of his head.

The latter was impossible.

Tonya haunted his thoughts and tortured his dreams.

The door to his therapist's office opened. "Hi, Foster. You can come back now," Marge said. "How are you?"

"Troubled."

"I don't like it when you start our sessions like that."

Foster took a seat on the sofa in the exact same spot as he always did. That gave him comfort. He set his coffee on the table and did his best to get comfortable. Nothing about therapy was easy. Sometimes his sessions weren't earth-shattering, but he knew this one would be gut-wrenching.

"What happened that has you conflicted?" Marge asked.

"A couple of things," he started. "The first one is Victoria. I found her with a big cut on her leg, which was infected. I managed to get her to the hospital, but she was wasted and by the time she sobered up, she wanted nothing to do with treatment."

"And what did you do?"

"I let her leave against medical advice, giving her a ride back to the alleyway she's been living in. I've gone back every day since then, but she's not there. None of her stuff is there and the guy that usually gives me information said she packed up, left, and didn't tell him where she was going. I've looked for her in all the usual places but no luck."

"How do you feel about that?"

"Deflated. Defeated. Guilty. I had promised Lisa I'd always look out for her mom. But I'm also tired. Victoria doesn't care about anything. I can't keep doing this. I know it's one of the things that keeps me living in the past."

"Just admitting that is progress."

He rubbed his chin. "I don't know that I can stop. I'm using it now to cope with something else."

"Wow. The fact that you can see that is huge. In the past, I'd have to guide you to that conclusion."

He chuckled.

"Does this have to do with Tonya?" She rested her notebook in her lap and arched a brow.

He'd spoken about Tonya before. His growing feelings that he would never act on. He once told Marge that if anything ever happened to Victoria, he wondered if he might pursue Tonya, but then quickly backtracked that conversation because he liked being alone.

"The last session we had, you mentioned that it was getting harder for you to separate your emotions," Marge said.

"It got worse when she asked me out and things got heated." Needing something to hold on to, he lifted his coffee. Part of him felt like he was kissing and telling. It didn't matter that he knew this was a safe space and Marge was required by law to keep their conversations private. "I care for her. I really do. But I can't give her what she wants and it wouldn't be fair to string her along and break her heart in a year or two."

"What did she have to say about this?"

"She agreed." A lump formed in Foster's throat. "Our short-lived love affair ended."

"Have you seen her since?"

He took a long sip of the brew he'd brought from the Green Bean down the street. "The first time was a wedding she sent my way. It was really awkward. We didn't know what to say or how to act around each other, but I want to be able to remain friends. I honestly can't imagine what life would be like if she wasn't around, but she wants kids and I can't go down that road again."

"Let's talk about that." Marge lifted her pen and jotted something down.

Whenever she did that, he wanted to know what she was writing, but he never had the balls to ask. He was sure it was her way of categorizing his words and thoughts so she could put them into his file for their next session. That's what a good therapist was supposed to do and Marge was the best.

"You've mentioned to me before that you never wanted to be in a relationship again because you didn't want the responsibility, but you tried it—for a hot minute—with Tonya. Only, the second it got real, you walked away because you don't feel you can do the family thing."

"I know I can't, and she knows that's a deal breaker for her."

"Is that what she said?" Marge arched a brow. "Or are those the words you put in her mouth?"

"She didn't disagree."

"All right. Now tell me what you said or what you were thinking about why you don't believe you want or can have kids. And be honest."

This wasn't the first time they'd had this conversation, but he'd never been totally truthful before. He'd always skirted around his real feelings because he could. There was no girl in his life so there was no reason.

"I've always told myself that I didn't have any more love for another child."

"That's not true and you know it."

He nodded. Love had nothing to do with it. That had always been his excuse. He thought he was being punished because he hadn't loved Lisa's mother. That cheating on Victoria had brought about Lisa's death somehow.

"So, what's the real reason?"

"I'm afraid I'll be a shitty partner like I was with Victoria. Or a terrible father. Or I'll resent another child because they aren't Lisa and no kid deserves that."

"No. They don't," Marge said. "But to be fair, you're not basing that on reality."

"What do you mean?"

"First. Didn't Victoria have two miscarriages after Lisa was born?"

"She did," Foster said. "I wasn't aware of the extent of her drug use at the time. After the second one, we stopped having sex altogether and I focused on doing my best to make sure Lisa was taken care of, but we know how that ended."

"You're deflecting," Marge said. "You were a good father. Having an affair doesn't make you a bad one, and what would have happened if Victoria didn't have a miscarriage and one of those children survived and was still here today?"

"Aren't you the one who constantly tells me not to what-if myself to death?"

Marge smiled. "I am. But humor me in this instance. How do you think you'd feel if you had a child who survived?"

"I don't know." He shifted in his seat, adjusting his jeans.

Marge didn't say anything. She just sat there and stared at him and that drove him crazy. A few long minutes ticked by while she waited for him to dig deep and get real.

"I'd probably love them."

"So why would having more children be any different?"

He glanced to the ceiling. "I feel like in some ways I'd be betraying Lisa, but mostly I worry I'd resent that kid, and then I'd end up hating its mother. Just thinking about it puts me in a bad headspace."

"I can understand your fears. What concerns me is how quickly you dismissed the relationship with a woman you have deep feelings for, especially when I know she's someone that you've worked hard to keep in your life."

"I still want that."

"What happens, say in a few months, when she's processed her emotions and starts dating someone? How will you handle that? Or fast-forward and put your head in the space where she gets married and has a family with another man. How are you going to cope with her moving on?"

Foster wanted to climb right out of his pants. His brain didn't want to conjure up that vision. It hurt his heart. The idea that Tonya would so easily allow another man into her life made Foster crazy jealous.

He didn't like that feeling.

"I have no idea," he admitted. "In the last few years, I've never seen her date anyone. I know she has, but I've been so isolated that it hasn't been in front of me. But I don't want to go back to where I'm living under a rock."

"Well, that's good news," Marge said. "However, I think you're selling yourself and her short. Not wanting to have a child because you just don't want them or because you're selfish and are focused on other things, I can accept. But your reasons are based in fear and things that have to do with the past. I'm not belittling your emotions. Far from it. I'm just saying that you haven't lived enough in the present to know whether it's something you want or not."

"I couldn't live with myself if I spent months with Tonya only to find out I'm never going to change my mind and that's the truth. The idea of having a child makes my heart race and not in a good way."

"Did you ever think you're hurting both of you by not fully allowing yourself to find out where you stand?"

"I did try," he said.

"A week or so isn't a relationship. And you allowed Victoria—your past—to dictate what your present would look like. That's not fair to yourself or Tonya."

"Are you suggesting that I didn't do the right thing by calling it off now?" He swallowed the bitter taste that smacked the back of his throat.

"You went from zero to eighty and then slammed on the brakes." She folded her hands in her lap. "I can't say one way or the other if having another child is for you. However, as your therapist of six years, you've never allowed yourself to explore the real reasons why you don't want to have one until now. Your fear isn't unreasonable, but it shouldn't be what stops you if it's something you want in your heart."

"I don't know if it is." He turned and stared out the window. "I have no desire to date anyone other than Tonya. There isn't anyone else out there who has even remotely turned my head. It physically hurts me that I can't give her what she wants."

"It's not that you can't. You're choosing not to, and I want you to really dig deep, past your fear, and see if there's another reason you're so willing to walk away from a woman who means so much to you."

"I know why." He glared. This was the part of therapy he couldn't stand. "I hate it when you make me repeat myself."

She wiggled her finger. "Nope. Saying you don't want to hurt her, while kind, it's still a cop-out. You're using her feelings to cover up your real issues and avoid what's going on in your world."

He raised his hands and slapped them down on his knees. "Okay. Why don't you tell me what you think."

"All right. We can do it this way." She leaned a little forward. "For a few days you got a taste of what it's like to feel good again. To live your life and that made you uncomfortable. You'd rather be miserable because you still believe you don't deserve to be happy. Being with Tonya and possibly having a family would require you to be present and to open your heart not just to others, but to yourself, and that there is the real problem. It makes you feel like you're forgetting about what happened. What you lost. Dressing it up like you're being a good guy and protecting everyone else, including a baby that doesn't exist, is bullshit."

Ouch.

"You've come a long way these last few years and proud of you for opening your heart, but you can't close it every time Victoria and the past rumble in because it will always be there," Marge said. "Is there any chance that you and Tonya can try again? Is that something you would be willing to explore?"

"I don't know how I feel about that. Especially since you're asking me to make her a guinea pig."

"You know that's not true." Marge tilted her head.

"Will you make an appointment to see me next week instead of waiting for our next session to discuss it?"

"You think I'm making a mistake?"

Marge stood, strolling across the room. She set her notebook down and leaned against her desk. "I don't normally make this kind of judgment, especially about this kind of thing, but yeah. I do. Here's the thing. If you decide to give things another try, you should tell Tonya why you pulled back, what you're afraid of, and why you're willing to give it a second go."

"That's a lot to think about."

"Schedule an appointment on your way out, okay?"

He didn't want to, which meant he knew he needed to.

The next seven days were going to be hell.

"Hey, old man. How's that arm?" Foster settled into the Adirondack chair in front of Maxwell's house. When Maxwell had called, Foster contemplated telling him he couldn't stop by, but there was no way he could do that to Tonya's grandfather. Whatever Maxwell wanted or needed, Foster would be there for the guy.

Although, after his session with Marge, he wasn't sure he could handle running into Tonya.

"If it weren't in this cast, I'd hit you right between the eyes." Maxwell arched a brow. "You made my favorite grandchild cry."

Shit. Not a great way to start a conversation. "I'd know better if I deserved that if I knew what Tonya told you."

"Nothing. She broke out in tears when I asked how you were, and then she refused to talk about it, so now I'm asking you."

"Is this why you asked me to come over and not to fix the bathroom fan?" Foster had wondered about that, but a few times Maxwell had asked him to be his handyman because he didn't want to burden his family. But Maxwell also generally wanted to discuss something with Foster that he didn't want his family to know. In the past, Foster was more than happy to lend an ear or drive him to a doctor's appointment without anyone knowing, but lately, it felt like a betrayal to Tonya. Especially now that Maxwell had been keeping the reasons for the visits from Foster.

"That's one of the reasons," Maxwell admitted. "I want to know what happened, and I'm begging you to be honest with me."

"No offense, old man, but isn't that between Tonya and me?"

"Of course it is, but I'm a nosy fool and I thought the two of you had finally figured out how good you are together."

Foster chuckled. "Does everyone around here believe we're a match?"

"Pretty much."

That shouldn't have come as a surprise. He glanced toward the sky. Maxwell had always proven to be a good listener and a safe space, only Foster had never discussed deep feelings about Tonya before. However, he had too much respect for the man to disregard his wishes. But that meant he had to discuss private matters and Tonya might not appreciate it. "Why else did you ask me over here?"

"I have another doctor appointment I need a ride to along with a personal meeting."

Foster shifted his chair, lifting his sunglasses to the top of his head. "I'll make a deal with you. If you tell me what's going on with your health, I'll tell you what happened between me and Tonya."

"That's emotional blackmail."

"Take it or leave it, old man."

"Fine," Maxwell scoffed. "You first."

"Nope. I know how you operate." Foster stretched out his arm. "But you have my word."

"Fair enough." Maxwell slumped in his chair. His eyes welled with tears. "I have cancer. It's terminal and I'm not going to fight."

"Jesus," Foster muttered. "Who knows about this?"

"Me. My doctors. And now you. And you're not going to tell anyone. They will want me to be poked and prodded and do whatever it takes. But I'm too old for that. I've lived a good life and I just want to go out on my terms."

Foster could respect that, but he didn't understand not sharing this news with the family. Especially one as loving as the Johnsons. "I won't say anything, but if confronted, I won't lie."

"That's reasonable and I know eventually I'll have to break the news, but not yet. I have another appointment that I need you to take me to."

"When?"

"Monday afternoon."

"I can do that," Foster said.

"Thank you. Now it's your turn." Maxwell tilted his head. "What the hell did you do to my grandbaby?"

Foster sucked in a deep breath. The rich pine from the trees filled his lungs. The sun dipped behind one of the big, puffy white clouds as it started to settle behind the mountains. The blue sky turned an orange-purple color. He took a few long moments to think about his answer. He'd spent the last few hours searching for Victoria and contemplating life, love, and family.

No one had seen Victoria since the night he'd found her with the cut on her leg. She'd come back to the alley, collected what few things she had, and disappeared. That wasn't totally unlike her, but she usually communicated with other homeless people where she was headed.

Not this time. Or at least they weren't telling him.

Every time she did something like this, he worried it would be the last time he'd see her alive. He knew that day would come and he didn't know what that would mean for his life. In some ways, Victoria gave him purpose.

And pain.

"I screwed up," Foster said. "I allowed my fears and my past to rule my decisions and pushed her away. Perhaps for good."

"When was the last time you spoke with her? Have you tried to mend things?"

"Nope. Because I didn't realize that I wanted to push through my issues until earlier today. But there's still a huge risk I could break her heart."

"That's true with any relationship," Maxwell said. "There are no guarantees in life. But if you don't risk it all, then you might as well crawl under a rock now."

"If that's true, why aren't you going to fight? Why are you giving up?" Foster knew that was a low blow.

"I've gone to two different specialists. Both have told me the same thing. My chances to live more than a few months are about ten percent. The treatments will suck the life out of me. I'd spend most of my time in hospitals and that doesn't sound fun. I'd rather enjoy what little time I have left living and enjoying my family." He tapped Foster's knee. "And maybe seeing some of my favorite people find the happiness that's been lacking in their lives."

"I know where you're going with that, and I care about Tonya. I really do. I want to call her and see if maybe she'll forgive my rash decision to cool it down, but my reason is a big one and she might not be so willing to give me a second chance."

"All you can do is ask." Maxwell pointed toward the path. "Might as well do it now."

"You sneaky old man."

Maxwell smiled. "I have my moments. Now help me to my feet so the two of you can chat."

Foster handed Maxwell his cane. He took a step back, giving him and Tonya a little space. Now all he had to do was find the right words and hope she gave him a second chance. "Should he walk up to your parent's house alone?"

"My dad is on his way down to get him." Tonya planted her hands on her hips. "Sorry he manipulated you into meeting me."

"It's fine. I'm glad he did. I want to talk with you."

"I see." She folded her arms. "Did you find Victoria? How is she?"

"I have no idea. I have a feeling it's going to be a month or so before she shows up again."

"Doesn't that concern you?"

"Of course it does, but I don't want to talk about her." Foster took Tonya's hand and tugged her toward the waterfront.

"Okay." She strolled down the path and up the stairs to the sundeck. Although, the sun was totally gone now and the stars had started to appear in the sky.

"We don't have to humor my grandfather," she said. "He means well, but you and I have said our piece."

Heartburn filled his chest, along with a large dose of fear. She had every right to tell him that it was best for her if they continued on their separate paths. He would respect it if that's what she wanted. "If he hadn't tricked us, I would have called you asking if we could get together." He tapped the switch for the lights, setting them to dim.

"Why?" She sat down on the lounge chair, bending her knees slightly.

He eased onto the edge, resting his hand on her ankle. "My emotions have been turned upside down and I understand that's no excuse for hurting you—"

"I told you before that you didn't hurt me."

He sighed. "But I did and what bothers me is I did so because I was afraid, not because everything I said was true, though I thought it was at the time."

"Foster, I'm okay. You don't have to worry about me."

"I'm sorry that I used what happened with Victoria to put a wedge between what was happening with us. I care deeply for you and your happiness is important to me. I know children is something you want and the fact that I'm not sure if I can give that to you—"

"We don't have to have a repeat of this conversation. We've said everything that needs to be said. It's time to move on."

"I know you're mad, but please let me finish," he said. He could absolutely understand why she was pissed, but he wanted a fair shake. "I'd like to try again."

"Dating?"

"Yes."

"Did you all of a sudden change your mind and want to get married and have a family?" she asked with a sharp tone.

This was not going as well as he would have hoped. "I don't know exactly how I feel about kids," he admitted. "I only know that I care about you and I want to be with you. I want to explore where it takes us. I know it's a risk and you were willing to take it with me before. I was hoping we could try again."

"No." She stood. "I'm sorry, but you were right. Kids are something that are not negotiable and I'm not willing to spend time in a relationship if that's not something you have no idea if you want. I don't regret putting my feelings for you out there. I would have never been able to move forward had I not done that."

"What are you saying?"

"We're not meant to be." She bent over and kissed

his cheek. "We'll always be friends. That's not going to change. I'll send business your way and I hope you will still do the same."

"Of course I will." His heart dropped to his toes. "Tonya. I don't understand. A week ago you were willing to take this journey with me."

"I've had some time to think about what matters to me and you're right. Kids are a deal breaker, so unless you can say without a doubt you're willing to have one in the future, I need to move on and find a partner who wants the same things as me." She turned on her heel and left him sitting there, stunned.

He shouldn't have been totally shocked or heart-broken, but watching her walk away left him with a hole in his soul.

One that he was going to do everything in his power to fix.

13

*T*onya hugged her sister, Tiki. She held on to her tight. The tears burned her eyes. "I'm so glad you're home." Tonya hadn't wanted to make girls' night all about her and her problems. She wanted to hear about Tiki and Lake's honeymoon and her next book. However, her heart still hurt over Foster. She tried to be strong, especially after seeing him at their grandfather's house yesterday, but her thoughts were all-consuming. Getting over him was going to be the hardest thing she ever had to do.

"Move over and let me get a squeeze." Tayla shoved Tonya out of the way and embraced Tiki. "You're positively glowing."

"We had such an amazing time." Tiki smiled from ear to ear. "I did miss you two crazy bitches."

"Of course you did." Tayla turned and opened a bottle of wine. "This might be the last time we can all drink together." She poured three glasses. "Gael and I are officially trying to get pregnant."

"That's so exciting," Tiki said. "Lake and I tossed birth control out the window, so you and me both."

Tonya swallowed. Mentally, she did a count of when she should get her period.

They had sex right after she finished her last cycle, so it would be a while. She didn't have the most regular period, but she couldn't tolerate the pill. She'd thought about going on other forms of birth control, but she didn't have a boyfriend, so she didn't have regular sex. She figured when that happened, she and whoever she was in a relationship with would discuss their options. After she and Foster had sex, she'd chosen not to mention the only form they'd used was the condom. That was enough for the time being. If things had progressed, she would have wanted to use something else. Condoms were a pain in the ass.

"This is so exciting. I'm so happy for both of you." Tonya raised her glass in a toast. She wanted to celebrate her sisters and how awesome it would be if they were both pregnant simultaneously. That would be spectacular. Utterly amazing. Her ovaries were on fire, thinking about the possibility.

The pressure to have a husband and children hadn't been at the forefront of her world until she hooked up with Foster, and then it all came crashing down. Part of her should have known that would happen. She loved Foster and she'd been in denial about that fact. Sleeping with him forced her to admit that to herself and by doing so, she had to accept that having a family was something she desired.

If she couldn't have it with Foster, she'd force herself to get past him and she'd open her heart to a man who would give her everything her heart craved. She knew it could happen. She'd witnessed it with other people in her life. Tiki for one. Her heart had been broken by her ex-boyfriend, Josh. But then she met Lake and everything changed; now they had the world at their fingertips.

And Tonya had never seen her sister so happy.

The same went for her other sister Tayla.

"Why don't we go sit outside," Tiki said. Lake and Tiki's house was spectacular. It overlooked Harris Bay and was about a mile down the road from where the girls had grown up. It was also a stone's throw from the carriage house where Tonya currently lived, which was nice because she could walk. It was a little farther for Tayla, but Gael and Lake were hanging out at Gael's place.

Unfortunately, they had invited Foster to join them. While they all knew that things hadn't worked out, she hadn't given them the details.

It shouldn't bother her that Gael and Lake invited Foster. The three men were friends and Tonya had to get past her negative feelings so she could maintain her friendship with Foster as well. That was more important than being butthurt over the fact that he was a broken man, incapable of being totally committed to another person.

She knew that when she made the decision to open her heart. She honestly didn't have regrets because she would have been stuck in limbo if she hadn't. She needed to have the experience so her mind and soul could move past this place she'd been living in for years.

"Should you two be drinking if you're trying to have babies?" Tonya plopped herself down on one of the big soft chairs in front of the gas fire pit. Everything about Lake and Tiki's house was so different from her folks. Lake had mad money.

Tonya wasn't judging. Her parents certainly weren't poor and growing up, she didn't want for anything. But Lake's wealth put new meaning into easy living.

So did Gael's, but he was more modest in the way he chose to live his life.

However, both her sisters were set up for life.

Tonya didn't resent that fact. She was grateful for that. Any nieces or nephews she had would have opportunities because of their station in life and she was sure their parents wouldn't spoil them too badly.

Her only issue at this point was that she had lost the man she loved. She could admit her feelings to herself now.

"My doctor said I should stop drinking, so this is my last night." Tiki held up her glass. "I wanted a night with my sisters and Lake agreed one more night of getting tipsy with the girls would be okay."

"Same with Gael and he was happy to have a night out with the boys." Tayla clanked her glass against the other two. "Although he mentioned Foster might be late. Something about him looking for Victoria."

Tiki reached out and took Tonya's hand. "I'm sorry. I wish things could have worked out with the two of you. I know how much you care about him."

"It's for the best," Tonya said. "I can't sit around and wait for him to figure out his life when I know what I want for mine."

"Wait. What?" Tiki shifted. "Are you kidding me right now? You waited years before you told him how you felt, and then you give up after a couple of weeks because he's a little wishy-washy over whether or not he wants to start a family again? That's your reason for ending it?"

"I think that's as good as any." Tonya blinked. She couldn't believe her sister's reaction.

"Not when you take freaking forever to tell the man you like him." Tiki lifted her glass and took a gulp. "That's not fair."

"You're being judgmental," Tonya said. "And for the record, he broke up with me the first time."

"The two of you dumped each other twice? How the hell does that happen?" Tiki asked.

Tonya wasn't going to explain it for the millionth

time. Everyone in her family needed to respect her decision. No one had wanted her and Foster to be an item more than she had, but it wasn't in the cards. "This topic is not going to be discussed anymore tonight."

Tiki lifted her hands, palms out. "I'm just trying to understand what happened while I was away."

"I was here, watching it, and I can't make heads or tails of it." Tayla crossed her legs. "I know Foster's confused as hell too."

"You talked to him about this?" Tonya turned her gaze to the lake. She couldn't fucking believe it. Her own sister talking about her behind her back and to Foster, of all people. She wouldn't have been so upset had it been with family. That she could understand. She was sure everyone had something to say about what had transpired between her and Foster. "Why would you do that?"

"We ran into him and it came up." Tayla tilted her head. "He told Lake that at first he thought it was the right move to break up, but not anymore."

"Did Mr. Big Mouth get into the details?" Tonya asked.

"Nope." Tayla shook her head. "Grandpa did."

Tonya closed her eyes and swallowed her pulse. She knew her grandfather meant well, but sometimes he could be a royal pain in the ass. "He doesn't have all the information and his opinion is tainted by Foster."

"Okay, then start talking, sister." Tiki sipped her wine before setting it on the small table between the chairs.

"There's nothing to tell." To prove her point, she raised her cell. "I re-established two dating apps, and I have one scheduled tomorrow night."

"No fucking way." Tiki snagged her cell and tapped at the screen.

Tonya should change her passcode. "Stop that."

"Do you remember what happened the last time you went on these apps? You ended up dating some creepy-ass men, not to mention that guy you had a crush on in the seventh grade who turned out to be a weirdo." Tiki swiped at the screen.

"Riley wasn't a weirdo," Tonya said.

"Oh. My God. You are not going out with Riley, the needy-ass fuck, tomorrow night." Tiki held up Tonya cell's phone. "What the hell are you thinking?"

"Give me that." Tonya snagged her cell. "He's a nice guy."

"He's needy as all get-out," Tayla said. "You had to have Grandpa and Dad explain to him that you no longer wanted to see him."

"You have to call off this date." Tiki arched a brow.

"I haven't confirmed it. He just saw that I was on the app again and messaged me, asking me out for tomorrow," Tonya finally admitted. She had no desire to see, much less be romantically involved with Riley.

But she did want to move past Foster. She spent years waiting for a man who couldn't give all of himself. It didn't matter that she knew without a shadow of a doubt that he cared deeply. Sometimes love wasn't enough.

"That does make me feel a little better," Tayla said. "But we both think you're making a mistake regarding Foster."

"Holy shit. You're kidding, right? This coming from the two people who thought I was crazy to sit around and wait for him." Tonya stood. She'd had enough. She loved her sisters, but it was time to call it a night. "I'm not going to sit here and do this with you. Not tonight. Not ever."

"Whoa. That's not fair." Tiki waved her hand and pointed to the chair. "We were the ones telling you to shit or get off the pot. We're glad you finally put it all out there. We're upset that Foster wants to try with you and you shut him down. That was cold."

"I love you both, but I'm walking home." Tonya downed the rest of her wine. No point in letting it go to waste.

"Don't be like that," Tayla said, but she didn't bother to get up. That was telling.

"Let her go." Tiki sighed. "Unless she's willing to have the hard discussion."

"I can't believe you." Tonya planted her hands on her hips. "Last year when you were going through all your shit with Josh, we were there for you and we certainly didn't judge you."

"Maybe so, but you did have a lot of opinions about what I should or shouldn't do. This situation is no different, except I listened to you," Tiki said. "You're not hearing anyone, and truthfully, you're being an asshole, especially to Foster, who wants to be with you. Josh didn't want to be with me. Big difference."

Tonya had no idea why her sisters were picking a fight. It wasn't the first time this had happened. Usually when it did, more alcohol had been consumed or it was about something a little heavier, but she had no intention of sticking around and playing along. She wasn't in the mood. Not tonight. Maybe never. Not where Foster was concerned. That was a closed book. "I'll see you both later." She waved her hand over her head and strolled toward the main road. It wasn't very late and it would take her all of ten minutes to get to the carriage house.

"Text us when you get home," Tayla called.

"Whatever," Tonya replied. Her chest tightened. She honestly tried not to regret her decision to be with Foster; however, it was becoming increasingly hard. Why everyone in her family took his side made no sense to her.

For starters, there shouldn't be a *side*.

Secondly, they should support her, not him. She understood they liked him and she didn't want that to stop. She still planned on trying to find a way back to being his friend.

But that would take time.

And space.

Perhaps a little patience.

Something her family should respect.

She turned down her street, rounding the corner past the Mason Jug, which was owned by Ryan's older brother and his wife. As she approached her carriage house, she groaned.

Foster's truck was parked in her driveway.

Shit.

He was the last person she wanted to deal with tonight, especially after this evening's events. She paused at the edge of the pavement. Her stomach twisted into knots. The realization that her sisters picked a fight with her and didn't fight to have her stay on girls' night because they knew Foster was waiting set her blood on fire.

He leaned against the back of his pickup with a bouquet of flowers.

The gesture was sweet. The anger flowing through her system shifted. She loved this man. She didn't like that he went to her sisters and concocted this ridiculous plan, but on the other hand, tricking her was the only way she was going to give him the time of day right now outside of work.

"What are you doing here?" She marched past him, doing her best not to make eye contact. She punched the code into the keypad. "And by the way, don't think for one second I'm inviting you in." If he pushed, she wouldn't say no.

"So, either I have to beg or stand out here like an asshole."

"I guess so." She glanced over her shoulder. "Except, I'll take those." She reached for the flowers. "They will look really nice on my kitchen table."

He yanked his hand away. "Nope. If you want these, we have to talk."

Loudly, she groaned. "Fine. Would you like a drink?"

"I'd love one."

"You can take a seat down by the waterfront. I'll bring you a glass of red. Does that work?"

"Bring the bottle because we're going to talk this all the way through." He arched his brow. "I'm not leaving until we do."

Tonya settled into the Adirondack chair and stared out over the lake. It was a warm night. No breeze. The few waves lapping against the breakwall came from boats humming down the shoreline. The dark sky was filled with a million stars. The curved moon hung high and shined bright.

However, her mood was as conflicted as a raging summer storm.

"I don't like how you used my family to get to me," she said.

"For the record, it was their idea and I protested."

She could feel Foster's gaze. It burned her skin. The emotions swirling between them ran as hot as they did cold. "Not hard enough."

"I was going to camp out here anyway. You don't answer my texts and sent my calls to voicemail. Take out the fact that I want more, we had decided that our friendship was important and we weren't going to let this get in the way of that."

She sighed. The latter had been a struggle. Her family adored Foster. The fact she spent a week with him and everyone knew it made it worse. They had all wrapped their arms around him and welcomed him into the fold. Of course, they had done that before, but it was worse now. "The first part of that statement makes the latter difficult."

"Bullshit," Foster said. "It's only difficult because you want more too." He leaned forward, setting his glass on the table. "Looking back on the way I behaved over the last year or so, there have been times I avoided you. I turned down invites to functions at your parents' house. Or volunteered to do extra jobs with Doug and Jim so that I didn't have to spend time alone with you because it was often hard. I told you it would be difficult to put the genie back in the bottle."

"Sometimes the way you make your point is annoying."

He chuckled. "I'm sorry I let my past and illogical thinking mess things up."

"Have you suddenly decided you want to have a family? Because I can't waste time with you if that's not something you believe could be in your future. It has nothing to do with our feelings for each other. I know you care about me, but I can't be with someone who doesn't want the same things as me, and I shouldn't have ever asked you to try. That was rude of me."

He reached out and took her hand, kissing the back side. "I'm scared. I never loved Victoria. The last year before Lisa died, I could barely look at her without feeling disgusted. I only stayed with her because Lisa loved her mother and begged me to protect her. I failed as a father."

"That's not true."

"Let me finish," Foster said. "This isn't easy for me to admit, but when I met Kathy, she made me feel alive. I didn't love her, but the excitement of being with her outweighed my good judgment. The night Lisa died, I had gone over to Kathy's. I had a babysitter at the house, but she had to leave and I told her I'd be home soon, so it was fine. Lisa was in bed and Victoria was passed out. Kathy talked me into staying for another round. I knew I shouldn't stay, but something was exciting and dangerous about it all."

Lifting her glass, she chugged her wine. It burned

going down. She poured another glass. She lifted it to her lips, but he took it. "Hey. I was drinking that."

"You've had enough for now," he said. "Do you understand why I blame myself for Lisa's death?"

"I've always understood that." She tucked her hair behind her ears. "You have to stop believing you could have controlled what happened. For all you know, you could have died that night if you had been there."

"Victoria didn't," Foster said with a straight face.

"Because she walked outside, sat down, and watched the fire. She had no idea what was going on. It was the neighbors who called it in. The police found her asleep in the backyard. You could have been in that house, just like your daughter." Tonya had never spoken those words before. Not to Foster. Not to anyone. She'd thought them many times. She was sure others had too, but no one dared to mention them to Foster. "I'm sorry. I know that sounds harsh and cruel."

"No. It's fine. It's not like Marge and I haven't discussed it before."

"Who's Marge?"

"My therapist," Foster said. "When I first started seeing her, it was all about learning to be grateful I was still vertical because I wanted to trade places with Lisa. I just knew that wasn't something that was possible. Since then, it's been about letting go of the past.

Marge believes it's all about letting go of my sense of responsibility for Victoria."

"I don't see you ever doing that and I went looking for her today. I came up with nothing."

"That was kind of you. I went to Saratoga and couldn't find her there either," Foster said. "You're right. I'm not sure I can completely forget about Victoria. I should. There are moments when the rage bubbles up and I don't understand why I help her, and then I think about Lisa. It's how I honor her memory."

"There are other ways you can do that." Tonya sucked in a deep breath, letting it out slowly. "You read the doctor's report. Victoria's hard living is going to cut her life short. What are you going to do when she's gone?" Tonya lifted her thumb to her mouth and chewed on her nail. This wasn't her business. This wasn't why he showed up with flowers.

But it was part of the problem.

"That's something I've been thinking a lot about the last twenty-four hours, along with some other things." He stood, lifted his chair, moved it to face her, and took her hands. "Outside of Victoria and Kathy and a few random girlfriends before my first wife, I don't have a clue about relationships. I don't know what it's like to be in love. All I know is I've never felt this way about another woman. It's terrifying and at the same time, it's exciting. That combination puts me in a weird headspace, and I keep pulling you in and pushing you away. I don't want to do that anymore."

"That's great. Only there's still one big problem."

"Kids," he said before she got the chance.

"Exactly. You're right. That is something that I'm not willing to negotiate on. Not for anyone. Not even you." She palmed his cheek.

"Here's the thing. My reason for not wanting a child is based in the same fear for not wanting to be with you and that's completely changed. I want this relationship to work. I'm more scared of the idea of losing you than I am of what it would mean to have a kid." He pressed his finger over her lips. "Most normal couples aren't discussing whether or not they're going to have kids together the first month into their dating."

"It's something that people put out there to know if they are compatible."

He nodded. "Let me put it to you this way. It's not off the table, but I thought maybe you could come with me to one of my therapy sessions sometime. We could talk about it."

Her jaw slacked open. A weird noise escaped her lips. "Excuse me? Did you just ask me to go to couples' therapy?"

He tossed his head back and laughed. "Not exactly. If you're not comfortable, I understand."

"I didn't say that. It's just that asking someone to do something like that speaks commitment."

Leaning in, he took her chin with his thumb and forefinger. He brushed his lips over her mouth in a sweet, slow kiss. "There are no guarantees. I'm not making any major promises. Only that I want to be with you and I'm willing to have the tough discussions."

Tears welled in her eyes. "You could still come to the conclusion you don't want children."

"The fact that I'm sitting here with you, begging you to take me back, I think it's safe to say that I'm leaning toward being okay with the idea." He dropped his forehead to hers and sighed. "No risk. No reward."

"It's mean to quote my grandfather to me in a situation like this." She snagged her glass and stood. "I must be crazy."

"Why?"

"Grab the wine," she said. "Let's go to bed."

"Are you inviting me to stay?' He jumped to his feet and stumbled a little, nearly falling over as he collected the rest of their things.

"I'm not going to repeat myself, Foster." She took long strides as she headed up the path. This could completely blow up in her face. However, she couldn't say no the moment he asked her to meet his therapist.

oster stretched. He hadn't slept that good in days. Weeks. Maybe even years. He was used to having haunting dreams that disturbed him to the point he was thankful for the jolt that woke him.

He rolled, reaching for Tonya, but she wasn't in bed. He found his cell on the nightstand. Six in the morning. He sighed. He needed to be at the Mason site by eight, and then he had five wedding rides.

A busy Saturday to say the least.

He should also go looking for Victoria.

But he was tired of being her keeper. He tapped the center of his chest. Marge had told him a dozen times that he'd kept his promise to Lisa. That there was only so much that he could do. He agreed. Victoria had given up on living a long time ago. He could keep telling himself that this time would be different. However, it was up to Victoria, and she spat in his face each and every time. He wasn't the person to help her.

He slipped from the bed, found his jeans, and hiked them up over his hips, not bothering to hook the button. "Tonya?" He padded down the hallway.

"In the kitchen," she called. "Shall I make you a mug of coffee?"

"That would be awesome." He smiled.

She stood with her back to him, wearing a long T-shirt that came to the middle of her thighs. Her hair was pulled back into a tight ponytail at the nape of her neck.

Wrapping his arms around her waist, he kissed her neck. "You're up early this morning."

"I've got two weddings; one has a bridezilla with a matching mother. It's all I can do to bite my tongue."

"Oh, wait. Is this the two o'clock boat drive that gave specific details for wave height?" He pressed himself against her body.

"That's the one."

"I told them I couldn't control the wind or the other boats on the lake and they told me I would lose my tip and they wouldn't pay me the rest of the deposit if I didn't make it happen."

She laughed. "What did you tell them?"

"That if they didn't like the conditions, we didn't have to go and I'd give them their money back, but they weren't getting on my boat without payment in full." His hands roamed the top of her thighs, easing under her shirt, lifting it up over her soft, round ass, slightly shocked she wasn't wearing any panties, but he wasn't complaining.

"What do you think you're doing?" She tilted her head.

He slipped his hand between her legs, teasing her gently with his index finger.

She groaned, dropping her head onto his shoulder. "I can't think straight when you do that."

"Good," he whispered. "That's the point." He cupped her breast with his other hand, pinching and twisting her tight nipple. He'd fantasized about her a number of times; however, she was so much more than he imagined. She was wild. Wicked. Incredible. Loving. Kind. Generous.

She was everything a woman should be and more.

He'd never experienced anything like her in his entire life.

Spreading her legs wider, he lowered his zipper and dropped his pants to his ankles. He desperately needed to be inside her. To feel her wrapped around him, holding him tight. He couldn't stop himself if he tried.

She accepted his length, pushing out her ass, grinding against him with a passion that made him drunk with desire. She gripped the counter with one hand and held on to his hip with the other, encouraging him to pump harder, faster.

He gritted his teeth as their bodies moved together in a dance that he never wanted to end.

"Yes," she said with a throaty moan.

He found her hard nub with his index finger and rubbed gently. It was wet and swollen.

"Oh, my God. Foster. Yes." She bent over the counter, raising her hips higher, glancing over her shoulder. Her climax gripped over him like a suction cup, pulling his orgasm from his body.

He shuddered.

She called out his name. Her body shivered. She reached up with both hands, clasping them behind his neck, arching her back, then releasing them as she fell forward, spent, gasping for breath.

Blinking, he tried to regain his composure as he smoothed his hand over her bare bottom. "That's a nice way to start my day."

Wiggling, she pulled down her shirt. "Better than coffee?" She pushed the button on the machine, while he managed to dress himself, again.

"You really have to ask?" He leaned against the counter.

"It was certainly unexpected."

"When you wear that." He wiggled his finger. "With nothing underneath. Don't ever think sex is off the table."

"Nope. Just on the counter."

He burst out laughing. "Over the counter. Next time we can try on it."

"Technicalities." She handed him a mug. Her eyes grew wide as she glanced down, then back up again. "Um, Foster. This is going to be a really gross question, but what happened to the condom?"

"What condom?" He tilted his head. His heart dropped to the pit of his stomach.

"The one you used."

"I didn't use one," he managed to croak out. The ramifications of her words smacked him right between the eyes. A slow burn filled the center of his chest.

"That was our only form of birth control."

"This was a conversation we should have had a while ago." He took his cup of Joe and made his way to the small table next to the kitchen. He sat down facing the window that looked out over the parking area and sighed. While he was ready to discuss his future, he wasn't prepared to deal with this. His stomach turned over. "Why didn't you stop me?"

She lowered her chin. "Are you serious right now? Every time we've had sex, we've used a condom. Why would I all of a sudden not want you to use one?"

"I don't know. It's been seven years since I've done this." He took a long sip of his coffee, letting the scalding brew burn the roof of his mouth. The desire to feel pain filled his soul, but he didn't want to hurt the same way he'd always wanted. Something in him had changed and he wasn't sure how he felt about that either. "There isn't anything we can do now other than wait this out."

"That's not true," she said. "I can get the Plan B pill."

Bile filled his mouth. "How does that even work? Is it safe for you? Are there side effects? Should you talk to your doctor first? I don't want you doing anything that would be harmful to you."

She cocked her head. "I would think you, of all people, would be jumping on this bandwagon."

He pinched the bridge of his nose. "I'm sorry, but I don't understand these things and I don't want you to do anything that would be detrimental to your health. Nor are we in a space where having a child would be good, even if I was on board with it."

"Which you're not."

"That's not true. It's just too soon." He closed his eyes. An image of Lisa filled his mind. She was maybe four or five and she was running around the backyard at night with his cell phone in her hand, using the flashlight, laughing hysterically. She was such a sweet little girl who loved life, even though hers was filled with constant heartache. For years, Victoria hid her drug use from everyone. The first couple years of their marriage, Foster thought their problems had to do with being young parents who suffered miscarriage after miscarriage. He ignored the signs. When he couldn't do that any longer, he did his best to make sure Lisa was protected by always having a nanny or babysitter on hand.

At first, Victoria didn't mind. She loved Foster's money and had no problem spending it.

"Hey. That wasn't meant as a dig." Tonya rested her hand over his. Her touch was soft and gentle.

He blew out a puff of air and leaned back. "I know. I was thinking about Lisa." If he wanted a relationship with Tonya, he had to be honest with her and that meant telling her about the tough things.

She held his hand tight. "You've never talked about her much."

"I'm not sure I'm ready to either," he admitted. "But I wanted you to know that's where my head was at." He stood and kissed her forehead. "I need to go take a shower and get ready for work. I'll stop at the pharmacy and look into this Plan B thing before I see you tonight. Is that okay with you?"

"Sure," she said. "But you don't have to do that. I can take care of it."

"Is it weird that I don't want you taking it without understanding what it's all about?"

"Yes and no," she said and nodded. "It's sweet you're concerned about me, but it's safe, so you don't have to worry."

"Is this something you've done before?" He shouldn't get upset even if she had.

"No. However, I have a friend who has, so I'm familiar with the process." She took his hand. "It's harmless. All it does is prevent me from ovulating and getting pregnant. It's not like it's causing an abortion or anything."

He brought her palm to his lips. "I'll pick it up and we can resume this conversation later. Right now, I better get my ass in gear." He stood and headed down the hallway toward the bathroom with conflicted thoughts.

On the one hand, he didn't want her to be pregnant. He wasn't ready for that. On the other, he didn't want her to take something to stop it either.

And that didn't make any fucking sense at all.

However, he remembered like it was yesterday the moment he found out Victoria was pregnant with Lisa. He and Victoria had broken up a few weeks before. He'd been ready to move on. Their relationship had been toxic and he was done. But he couldn't turn his back on *his* child.

Nor his baby's mother.

He wasn't *that* man.

And he would never be that kind of person.

"Hey, Doug, do you have a minute?" Foster tossed his work belt into the back of his truck. He glanced at his watch. He had fifteen minutes before heading back to his place, giving him enough time to shower and change so he could make it to the docks in time for the first wedding ride.

"Sure." Doug jogged across the gravel. "What's up?" He leaned against the cab, wiping the sweat from his brow. His long dark hair touched the top of his shoulders.

"This will be an awkward conversation I hope we can keep between us."

"Whatever it is, you don't have to worry. You can trust me." Doug nodded.

"This will be a personal question, and if you don't want to answer, I understand." Foster squared his shoulders. "When your first wife told you she was pregnant, did you ever consider not getting married? Or not having the baby?"

"No. Why?"

"I didn't either." Foster let out a long breath. "But I also hadn't known we had gone without birth control."

"Shit. How did that happen? If you don't mind me asking. I mean, Jim and Stacey's mom were in high school. They were dumb kids. I was a grown-ass man and our birth control failed."

"Victoria had a horrible habit of forgetting to take her birth control pills, but she had no problems taking drugs."

"That's a tough one," Doug said.

"Yeah." Foster nodded. He hadn't thought this

conversation through well since there was no easy segue into the next part, so he was going to toss it out there. "What about the Plan B thing? Could it have been an option for you and Mary or was it too late or did you not want to use it and do you know anything about it?"

Both of Doug's eyebrows shot up. "Okay, because I can't imagine you asking if this wasn't important to your personal life, no, it wasn't an option. And even if it was, at that time in my life, I thought I loved Mary. I honestly wanted that child, and the whole reason we filed for divorce was that she decided having a family right away wasn't part of her plan, and then she had an affair. But I have to know why you're asking."

"That's a reasonable request," Foster said. "Unfortunately, I'm not going to answer that. However, I do have one more question."

Doug chuckled. "Shoot."

"Do you know if it's safe?"

"I have no idea. That would be a question for my wife." Doug raised his hand. "Who has never taken it, but she's up on all these female things." He reached in his back pocket and pulled out his cell. "Hold on one second. I have to take this." He tapped the screen and held it up to his face. "Hey, pumpkin. How's daddy's little girl?"

"Mommy says I have to go fishing tonight. Why do I have to go? I hate fishing."

Foster did his best not to laugh at the cute sound

of the little girl's voice at the same time it tugged at his heartstrings.

"Because it's Brandon's turn to decide what we do on family night. When it's your turn, he has to do whatever you want."

"Well, I pick going to the hair salon."

Doug groaned. "You know that's not on the approved list, sweetie."

"Daddy. That's not fair. Fishing should be on that list."

"Fishing doesn't—honey, we'll talk about this when I get home, which will be in fifteen minutes. Okay."

"Fine." The phone went dead.

"How old is your daughter?"

"Nine." Doug shook his head. "And she's a little freaking princess. I thought being sandwiched between two boys she'd be all rough and tumble like her mom. Jim is in grandpa heaven because Stacey was never like this. She was a little tomboy and Heidi is all girl. It's kind of scary. Stacey doesn't know what to do with her half the time and neither do I. All I know is thank God my wife is still packing because when the boys start coming around, she's going to scare them all off."

"Um, man. You're like the jolly green—"

"That joke is so fucking old, it's not funny." Doug slapped Foster on the shoulder. "Look. I get your entire world is changing. I've been there. Perhaps different circumstances, but it can be chaos at times. We're going to renovate your home and waterfront. That's a big deal. You're officially working for us full-time, taking on different responsibilities. And you've been dating when you haven't done that in years. I know Tonya means a lot to you and whatever prompted this conversation, knowing you, it's hitting you right in the center of your soul."

Foster took in a deep breath. "That's about right."

"Can I give you a piece of advice that might not go down easily?" Doug asked.

"Sure."

"Stop overthinking and just live. Enjoy all the moments. All the risks. All the insanity that comes with being in love, which by the way is sloppy as hell. Nothing about this should be too planned out. As a matter of fact, all the best things about mine and Stacey's life are all those things that happened without us trying. So, sit back, relax, and enjoy the ride."

"I wish I could be like that."

"You can be. It's a choice. A mindset. It takes a while to get there. I know I couldn't until after Mary's murder was solved, but after that, life just became too short to worry about all the other things," Doug said. "Do you love Tonya?"

No one had ever point-blank him that. Not even Maxwell. "I think I do."

Doug placed his hand in the center of Foster's chest. "There's no thinking involved when it comes to love. With every beat of your heart, she's there. That emotion sits in your soul. And speaking from experience, it's different from the love you have for your kids. Brandon, Heidi, and Dallas are the oxygen I breathe. The water I drink. But Stacey's my compass. Some people say the person you marry—or your partner—is a choice. I agree with that to a point. However, Stacey's my world and based on the circumstances that brought us together, we are meant for each other. I believe if you search your heart, you'll come to the same conclusion for you and Tonya."

"Anyone ever tell you that you're a sappy old man?"

"My wife. Every day." Doug smiled. "I'll see you on Monday."

Foster climbed into his truck and leaned across to the passenger side, opening the glove box. He pulled out a picture of Lisa and traced his fingers over her beautiful face. He missed her so much. Tears filled his eyes. She would have been fifteen now. He tried to imagine what she would look like. Dropping his head back, he closed his eyes for a long moment.

Loving Tonya didn't make him ready for anything other than a relationship.

Only, he had acted like a horny teenager, putting parenthood on the line. He was going to have to learn more about this Plan B pill. He shouldn't be this conflicted. He couldn't replace his sweet girl. That was impossible and he didn't want to.

But Doug was right about where his emotions began when it came to Tonya and they weren't going away. They grew stronger every day and he wanted to give her the things she valued most.

He was going to be thirty-eight on his next birthday. He wasn't getting any younger. He needed to come to terms with the fear that controlled his inability to move past this one hurdle before it was too late.

15

*T*onya strode down the dock toward Foster, where he paced back and forth, obviously agitated about something, but she had no idea what. He'd texted, stating he needed to talk, although he hadn't elaborated. All he would give her was that it was important and needed to be discussed immediately.

The first wedding ride went off without a hitch. The bride and groom were ecstatic. The second couple had been a little more high-maintenance but still enjoyed themselves. However, in the last twenty minutes, Foster's mood had soured dramatically, and it had nothing to do with their concerns over their poor choice this morning in the kitchen.

He glanced up when she was ten feet away. "I've got to go. Can you handle the ride around the bay, and can I borrow your car?"

"Yes, to both counts, but how do you expect me to get home?"

He glanced over his cell. "You can't drive my boat back to my place? That's what I would have done. You can either stay at my place or take my truck, and I'll meet you at your place later."

"What's going on?" She curled her fingers around his biceps. "You're white as a ghost."

"It's Victoria. She's in the hospital. It's not good."

"I'll go with you."

"No. These are your clients. Neither one of us should cancel. Besides, she's all the way up in Ticonderoga."

Tonya swallowed. Victoria never went north. Only south. For her to do that meant she hadn't wanted to be found. Part of Tonya could understand why. Victoria had made it clear more than once she was tired of Foster interfering with her life. There had been times when Victoria told him she wanted to be left alone and planned on leaving the state so he couldn't find her again. Other times she made it clear she needed money, not food.

"Let me call Gael and Lake. They can come to get the boat and return it to your home. We can go up together after the ride."

Foster shook his head. "There's no reason for you—"

"Are we a couple?"

"Yes," he said.

"This is what girlfriends do."

His eyes were wet with tears. "I've got to call her parents. I've been told she's at end of life. I'm not sure I know what that means."

A sudden chill snaked through Tonya's bloodstream. "Foster. I don't want you driving up there alone. You're obviously distraught." She pulled out her cell. "We'll do this ride together and I'll make sure your boat is taken care of." She glanced over her shoulder. "We'll call her parents on the drive to Ticonderoga. Okay?"

"You're not going to let me say no, are you?"

She shook her head.

"Thank you." He leaned in and kissed her cheek.

Pressing her hand against the center of his chest, she said, "You never have to thank me for supporting you."

The last thing Foster wanted was Tonya to be here during the perfect trifecta for a shitshow.

If he thought Victoria could be cruel sometimes, her parents could be worse.

Add Kathy into that mix, and this situation could become toxic in minutes.

It wouldn't matter that Victoria could be on her deathbed, Victor and Denise considered their child dead anyway.

They also hated Kathy. Not because of his affair with her, but because of the condescending attitude she'd had with them when Lisa had fallen off her bike before they knew he'd been messing around.

He did his best to keep his blood pressure in check as he made his way down the corridor. The lovely people in the emergency department had informed him that Victoria had been admitted and was currently in the ICU where she was on a ventilator. After she was released from prison, her parents wanted nothing to do with her and he agreed to be responsible. Ever since then, he was listed as having power of attorney. He could have forced her into rehab, which he'd done once before.

But she walked out three days after she'd been admitted.

Not worth doing it again.

Foster had continued to offer it. He continued to drag her to meetings. Shelters. Other services that could better her existence. But overall, Foster had to come to terms with the idea that he'd done his best to live up to his promise to his daughter.

Tonya grabbed his arm. "You haven't said five words to me since we left the Village. I'm worried about you and how you're handling all this."

"I'm still processing the news and trying to figure out how to deal with Victor and Denise. If they are even here."

"Oh. We're here," a familiar male voice bellowed.

Foster paused in front of a waiting room of sorts, shocked that they had beat him to the hospital. They were about a half an hour farther south than he had been and knowing them, they took their time leaving their house. He leaned closer to Tonya. "Why don't you go get some coffee and snacks." He pulled out his wallet and handed her a twenty.

"I'm not leaving your side."

"Your heart is in the right place, and I adore you for it. But I need to speak to them alone." He kissed her forehead. "Please."

"Okay. But I'll be right back."

"Thank you." He took a few moments to collect his thoughts before stepping into the small room.

An ugly blue sofa sat in front of a window. A table with four chairs was positioned in the center of the room while a small television hung in the corner.

"To be honest," Foster started, "I'm surprised you both made it." He stuffed his hands in his pockets and shifted his gaze between Victor and Denise. There was no love lost between his in-laws anymore. They resented him for his support of their daughter, not the death of their grandchild. They didn't hold him responsible for that the same way he held himself. "You've told me that if it ever came down to something like this, you'd let me deal with it, which I'm doing."

"You called us, remember," Victor said, wrapping his arm around his wife.

"As a courtesy. I felt you deserved to know what was going on. I'm sorry if I made it sound like I expected you to be here to make any decisions."

"You didn't," Denise said. "Kathy did. She called us first. We were on our way here when you called, arguing over whether we should call you before we got here."

"Excuse me?" Foster arched a brow. He knew Kathy worked at this hospital when she wasn't working at urgent care, but why the fuck would she call Victoria's parents? She knew they wanted nothing to do with their daughter. "I knew she was here tonight, because she's the one who informed me that Victoria came into the ER, but I had no idea she called you. As a matter of fact, you're not even on Victoria's next of kin list, no offense."

"None taken." Victor swiped at his eyes.

"Tell him, Victor," Denise said softly.

Victor let out a long breath. "Kathy told us that you asked her to call. I know that's not true."

"No. It's not." Foster had no idea what game that woman was playing, or why. Frankly, he wasn't sure he wanted to find out. "I'm sorry she did that. I can't for the life of me fathom her reasons."

"I can," Denise said. "She thinks bringing us together will be the catalyst that brings the two of you back together."

"That's the dumbest thing I've ever heard," Foster said under his breath. "I've barely seen her since

Victoria went to prison. When I have, it's never been good. What the hell is she holding on to?"

"Maybe her own guilt," Victor said.

Foster arched a brow. "I don't believe that for one second. Not based on my conversations with her, but honestly, she's the last person I want to talk about. Victoria is who we should be focusing on. You should know that I had taken her in for a cut on her leg and it was infected. She left against medical recommendation and disappeared. I didn't push as hard as I should have or as I have in the past."

"No one expected you to." Victor squeezed Foster's forearm. "The last seven years have been difficult for all of us and this isn't the outcome we wanted. Of course we wished our daughter would have gotten help, but when she showed no remorse for her actions that led to Lisa's death, that's when we as parents had to walk away. It wasn't to hurt you; we know you've suffered so much."

Foster held up his hand. "I've never blamed you for anything."

Denise inched closer. "We've always loved you and never wanted to push you away, not even when we learned of your affair."

He grimaced. "That wasn't my most shining moment and I'm sorry that my mistake is once again shoved in your face."

"You were stuck in a bad marriage. All you did was pick the wrong woman to try to move forward with," Denise said. "We don't know what Kathy's motives are for calling us tonight and frankly, we don't care. We're sorry to leave that at your feet. We're here to beg you to put all of us out of our misery and not take any heroic means when it comes to Victoria."

"You have control," Victor said. "This is your decision, but as her parents, please, end her pain. End it all for us. You can extend her life for weeks, maybe even a month or so, but what purpose would that serve?"

"I haven't spoken to her doctors. Only the ER ones and they told me she was in organ failure. I'm not sure I understand exactly what that means or how that happened. What have they told you?" Foster stuffed his hands in his pockets and made his way to the window which had a view of the parking garage.

Wonderful.

Well, at least he could see some blue sky. That calmed his soul a little.

"My understanding is that her liver and kidneys aren't functioning properly, but that's the easy part of her issues. She went into cardiac arrest. She was dead for four minutes. While she has some brain activity, even if she can breathe on her own, she might not ever be herself again."

When Foster first met Victoria, they'd been in their late teens. She was already into her addiction, but it had been far from apparent. She'd been vibrant.

Fun. Full of life. Not this shell of a human he'd known since shortly after Lisa had been born.

"You're asking me to take her off the ventilator and let her die," Foster said softly.

"Yes. It's honestly the most humane thing any of us can do." Victor stood beside him, resting his hand on his shoulder. "You've looked over her for seven long years. You've given up starting your life over. You could have fallen in love, gotten married, had a family. Instead, you chose to be her guardian angel. She probably would have died years ago had it not been for you."

A guttural sob caught in his throat. "I don't know if that's a good thing or a bad thing."

"It's both," Denise said. "That young woman you came with. The wedding planner. She means something to you."

"She's been a good friend for a long time," Foster admitted.

"She's more than that," Victor said. "Letting go of Victoria doesn't mean you're letting go of Lisa."

Tears flowed freely from Foster's eyes down his cheeks. Not once had he ever voiced those words. He hadn't even allowed himself to think it. The few times his therapist had brought it up, he waved it off like the thought was an annoying fly on the wall. If Marge pushed the agenda, he brushed it under the rug, holding on to the promise he'd made to his daughter.

That was the only reason.

Not the fear his precious memories would vanish in a cloud of smoke.

"I found decent coffee, but the snacks are basic." Tonya's voice filled his heart like a much-needed hug.

He turned, swiping at his cheeks.

She set a tray on the table in the center of the room and tilted her head.

Everything around him disappeared. The only thing he saw was Tonya. He closed the gap and wrapped his arms around her, resting his chin on top of her head. Her hair smelled like strawberries. He inhaled sharply, unable to get enough. "Thank you," he whispered.

"I have no idea for what, but okay." She held him tight.

"Victor. Denise. You're right. It's time. I'll talk to the doctors and ask them to take her off the ventilator."

Victor curled his hand over Foster's biceps. "It could be hours. It could be days. But we'll get through this together."

16

"So, how long have you and Foster been an item?"

Tonya swallowed as she tried to come up with the perfect words to answer Denise. Everything still felt so complicated with Foster.

"It's new." Tonya uncrossed her legs and shifted in her seat. Victor and Foster had left the waiting room to have a discussion with hospice care. Victor thought Foster was nuts to bring Victoria back to his place if she survived having the breathing tube pulled out, which the doctors didn't think would last more than a few hours.

But they couldn't be sure.

Anything was possible.

However, Foster was adamant that if she could be released and die anywhere but a hospital, that would be what was best for Victoria.

Tonya would support him no matter what. She loved him and he was doing what he thought was best. He was a compassionate man who suffered a great loss and all he wanted was a bit of peace in his life.

"Is that code for you don't know what the hell is going on?" Denise leaned forward, resting her hands on the table.

"I wouldn't go that far."

"When Victoria was in prison, we gave Foster space. He was angry at the world, but he internalized it. We always believed we'd eventually have a good relationship with him again, but then he started enabling Victoria."

"I don't mean to be disrespectful, but he doesn't see it that way."

Denise nodded. "I know. However, he was driven by guilt for his affair. He's always believed that Lisa would be alive if that hadn't happened. Even though we don't hold him responsible, or even Kathy, whom I can't stand, Foster did stay out that night and that's a dark cloud that's nearly impossible to get out from underneath."

"If he'd been at home, he could have died too."

"That's a true statement and no one wanted that either." Denise took Tonya's hand. "We've missed having Foster in our lives. He's a good man with a big heart. But to us, Victoria died a long time ago. We told her when she got out of prison that if she was ever serious about getting help, we'd be there for her. Foster knew that we wouldn't turn our backs on her if she was willing to do the work. But we couldn't have our hearts broken again."

"I can understand that."

"You seem like a sweet, caring person. Foster deserves to have someone who will love and cherish him. Promise me that you will help bring us together and keep the memories alive." Denise sniffled.

"You're Lisa's grandparents. Why would I ever want to stand between you and Foster? I know how much keeping a connection with his daughter means to him, so I would never do that. I just don't know if Foster and I will ever be more than ships passing in the night."

"I've known Foster since he was in high school. He's never looked at a woman the way he looks at you." Denise smiled and patted Tonya's hand. "He's a wounded man. But he's not broken. His heart might have a part that will always be filled with pain, but that doesn't mean the rest of it can't be filled with happiness. He's held on to Victoria because he thought that was the only way he could keep his love alive for Lisa."

"It's not just that," Tonya said. She'd understood that about Foster for years. "He believes that if he has a life, if he falls in love or starts any part of his life over, then he's stomped on Lisa's memory. It's as if staying in limbo allows him to stay with Lisa at the exact instant of her death. But if he moves forward, then he has to accept she's really gone."

The sound of someone clearing their throat caught her attention. She glanced up.

Foster stood in the doorway with a scowl.

Shit.

"Excuse me. I should go find my husband." Denise stood and scurried out of the room.

"What the hell was that?" Foster folded his arms and glared. "I don't appreciate you psychoanalyzing me with my mother-in-law."

She loved how he used the term mother-in-law to reference Denise. He hadn't used that word in years. Of course, Tonya knew Foster cared for Victor and Denise. He always spoke fondly of them, even when he disagreed with their decisions.

"Are you going to tell me it's not true?" Tonya had been biting her tongue when it came to Foster and his daughter. She'd done so out of respect and it had been none of her business.

Now that they were a couple, she believed things were different. She should be able to talk about her feelings and opinions. Hell, he'd invited her to one of his therapy sessions.

"You shouldn't be discussing it with Denise."

"Are you mad about that? Or because I hit a nerve?" Her heart raced. She stood, inching closer.

He narrowed his stare. "You have no idea what it's like to suffer a loss like that. How dare you think it's okay to even question where my head is at or what I think this might mean."

"Don't go there, Foster." She kept her distance to a safe two feet away. She knew better than to get in his space right now. "I might not live your experience. I accept I haven't a clue. But don't you dare pull this bullshit with me again." Fuck it. She closed the gap and poked his chest. "You are not going to pull me in and thank me for God knows what and then push me away because I express what I'm thinking and feeling. Maybe I shouldn't have said that to Denise, but you don't make it easy to have deep, meaningful conversations about the things that matter in your life. I love you, Foster, and I can't stand by and watch you torture yourself anymore. Not when my heart is paying the price. I put myself out there. I put it all on the line. It's your turn to get real."

His mouth slacked open and he said something, but she wasn't sure what it was because her adrenaline burned hot and her lips kept moving. Years of pent-up emotions spilled out.

"I don't expect you to do it all at once. I know my timing sucks with what's going on, but you can have your past. You can have loss and grief and all the things that go with it. You've spent time with my grandfather. He lost a child. He feels that pain every day. But he also cherishes life. He loves deeply. And most importantly, he found a way to have a present and a future." She took his hand and placed it in the center of her chest. "I could be that for you if you'd open your damn eyes and heart." She let out a long breath. "I'll call one of my sisters to come get me. Let us know if you need anything." She raised up on tiptoe and kissed his cheek. "Figure it out, Foster. I'm only going to be around for so long."

With tears burning her eyes, she strolled down the long, bright corridor toward the elevator.

Foster didn't chase after her.

That spoke volumes.

She pulled out her cell and texted both her sisters. It was a big ask, but one of them would take pity on her and make the drive to Ticonderoga.

Tiki was the first to respond. With a phone call.

"Hello," Tonya answered, leaning against the wall. "You could have texted me back."

"What's going on? I thought you planned on staying with Foster until either she passed or he took her home."

"It's a long story and one I don't feel like getting into at this moment," Tonya said.

"I can be there in forty minutes, but you're really going to leave him?"

"Let me put it to you this way. He didn't chase me out of the building."

"I don't know what that means," Tiki said.

"I'll explain it when you get here."

"All right. See you soon." Tiki ended the call.

As Tonya wandered the halls of the hospital, she came upon a pharmacy.

Plan B pill.

She sighed as she stepped inside the store. She snagged a soda, some chips, and strolled to where she thought she might find the dreaded little pill. She scanned the shelves.

Condoms.

Sponges.

Pregnancy tests.

Finally, she found what she was looking for. She picked up the package and stared at the words on the front. Never in a million years did she think she'd be in this position with Foster, of all people.

"Oh. Hello," a female voice said. "Tonya, right?"

Shit.

"Where's Foster?" Kathy asked. "Why aren't you with him?"

This was none of Kathy's business and she certainly wasn't going to discuss it with the likes of her. Part of Tonya could understand why Foster had been upset over her blubbering to Denise. Or to anyone for that matter.

However, it wasn't like she'd confided in a stranger. At one point, he'd been close to Victoria's parents and had he chosen to deal with his ex-wife differently, they still might be.

"I've got a question for you." Tonya might as well

go for broke. If Foster knew she was doing this, he'd really be pissed. "Why did you call Victoria's parents?"

"I think the answer is obvious."

"Actually, it's not," Foster's voice startled Tonya.

She jumped, dropping the box that she'd been holding to the floor.

"In part because you lied to them." Foster bent over, lifting the box into his hands and fiddling with it.

Tonya's heart raced. Her eyes stayed focused on the words on the cardboard and their meaning.

"I have no idea what you're talking about." Kathy dared to reach out and touch Foster's bicep.

He recoiled.

Kathy scowled. "Victoria is dying, Foster. Her parents have the right to know that and be by her bedside."

"No, actually, they don't. They gave up that right a long time ago. What happens to Victoria is on me. The only person you should have called was me and you know that. But more importantly, you interfered in my relationship with them by lying. Why?"

"There's no need to raise your voice with me," Kathy said. "Let's take this where we can talk privately."

Foster looped his arm around Tonya's waist. "Anything you have to say to me, you can say in front of my girlfriend."

Kathy gave Tonya the once-over.

Tonya shivered.

"I'm sorry. I don't see the attraction, but whatever." Kathy shook her head. "Five minutes. Give me five minutes of your time. That's all I ask."

"Just say what's on your mind." Foster let out a long breath.

"All right, but for the record, I didn't want to do this in front of anyone." Kathy folded her arms across her middle. "Do you remember the night I called you from urgent care about three months after the fire?"

"Nope. We're not doing this again, Kathy." Foster shook his head. "You have tried to bring that up more than once. If it is true, then I'm sorry that happened to you, but that doesn't tie us together. Not the way you would like it to. We're over. Let it go."

Kathy planted her hands on her hips. "You threw away the best thing that ever happened to you."

"That would be Tonya, and I plan on making sure that doesn't happen."

"Well then, maybe you might want to talk her out of taking that pill." Kathy waved her hand over her head and turned on her heel. "Or maybe you could break her heart and she'll miscarry too."

"What was she talking about?" Tonya swallowed. "She lost a baby? Your baby?"

"So she claims."

"And you don't believe her?"

"I don't believe much of what comes out of her

mouth, especially when she wouldn't provide the details." Foster lifted the box.

She glanced up. "What does that mean?"

He continued to examine the product as if it were a fine piece of jewelry. He held it up to the light and then brought it closer to his face. He squinted. "I was always super careful about using protection. I was married and I didn't want to be put in a position where I had another child. That would be a betrayal to Lisa that I couldn't handle. It was bad enough I was cheating on her mother. Kathy always said she was on the pill, but maybe she wasn't. That's always possible, but I not once went without a condom."

"You did with me," Tonya said.

"That's true. However, I never once went without with Kathy. Not that this is an excuse, but I hadn't had sex in seven years." He made eye contact. "You said you loved me."

She blinked. She'd said a lot of things during her rant and those words had flown from her lips like a runaway train. She wanted to take them back, but she couldn't. There were out there in the universe forever.

"I might have."

"No. You did." He put the box on the shelf and took her by the shoulders. His intense eyes tore deep into her soul. "I heard it clear as day. I'm not sure I heard anything after that and you certainly didn't hear me."

"You didn't say anything."

He took her chin with his thumb and forefinger. "I tried to. But you bulldozed right over me. I'm not used to you being assertive. I like it." He brushed his mouth over her lips in a tender kiss. "What you failed to hear was me telling you that I love you too."

"Don't mess with me. I'm not in the mood."

He chuckled.

"This isn't funny."

"Your response to me is." He took her by hand and led her out of the pharmacy.

Without the Plan B pill. She glanced over her shoulder. "We should purchase that now."

"We have a day or two from what I've read," he said. "Stop deflecting from the conversation we're having right now."

"Okay. You let me walk away earlier."

"Not really." He led her to the elevator. He pushed the button and waited. "I had every intention of coming after you, but the doctor came in and I had to deal with that before searching for you."

"You overreacted to what I said to Denise, although I will admit that I might have overstepped."

"You're right about what I'm afraid of."

The elevator doors swung open, but neither one of them entered. They stood there in the middle of the hallway, staring at each other.

"I will never ask you to forget Lisa. Or Victoria. Or any part of your past," Tonya said. "All of that makes up who you are. I'm not looking to change you."

"I know that." He nodded. "But my fears aren't going to go away overnight just because I've voiced them."

She palmed his cheek. "I'm not asking for it to go away. I'm only asking that you make room in your heart for me."

"I love you. I've been afraid of that too. As if all this change somehow means Lisa won't be part of my life. Deep down I know that's not true." He took her hand and placed it over his chest. "As far as that box I put back on the shelf, well, I'm afraid if we don't take it, we're rushing into things we're not ready for and all my fears will be put into play. But I'm also afraid if we do take it, I'm not moving forward at all. I want to live. I want a life with you. I don't know what that looks like; I just know that my life is better with you in it."

"We have a day or two before that pill isn't an option," Tonya said. "We can talk more about it when we're both less emotional."

He leaned forward and hit the button for the elevator again. "We need time to be a couple. Knowing each other—being close friends—isn't the same."

Stepping into the enclosed space, she wrapped her arms around him, leaning into his strong body. She stared into his sweet, loving eyes and for the first time, she saw her future. "There's a lot going on right now."

His lips brushed over her mouth as the doors closed. "I promise I will give all of me to this relationship, but I need to deal with Victoria."

"I'm here for you. Whatever you need me to do."

"You might not like this part, but if it's possible, I want to bring her home with me."

She palmed his cheek. "Of course you do. And you're going to sit by her side right to the end. I'd expect nothing less."

"Thank you," he whispered. "I know this is asking a lot, especially since you haven't always agreed with how I handle Victoria."

"I've only wanted to be there for you." She smiled. "And that's what I'm going to do." She knew they would weather whatever happened next because they had each other.

Foster rested one hand gently over Victoria's pale wrist while he gripped Tonya's with his other.

Victoria's parents stood on the opposing side, staring at their daughter while she breathed on her own. She could survive for a few more days, but the doctors said it wouldn't be long. They had her doped up, so she'd be comfortable. There was no reason for her to suffer. All her organs were failing. It wasn't the infection that had killed her—although that had been her final nail in the coffin.

The doctors had removed the breathing tube and taken Victoria off all the machines.

"Let me go see what's going on with the discharge papers and where that wheelchair is," Tonya said softly.

"Thank you." Foster leaned over and kissed her temple. He jumped when someone pulled the curtain back.

"I wanted to check on everyone and see if there was something I could do." Kathy stepped into the room. "I know this is a difficult time and if I can be of service, I'm happy to help."

Foster stiffened his spine. It was as if history was repeating itself. He swallowed the bile that had bubbled up from his gut. A flash of seven years ago burned in his mind. He could see Kathy stepping into the hospital morgue after he'd said his final goodbye to his precious Lisa. Victor and Denise hadn't known who Kathy was at the time, and he thought she'd have enough respect for him—and them—to keep it that way.

Unfortunately, Kathy had another agenda. She went in as if she were a concerned medical professional and then dropped the bomb, nearly destroying his already tense relationship with Victor and Denise.

"This is no place for you." Victor stepped to the

edge of the bed. He puffed out his chest. "You aren't welcome. Please leave."

Tonya caught Foster's gaze. Her nose crinkled like it did when she was puzzled. He'd told her some of what had gone down with Kathy. The restraining order. The harassment he'd endured because she wouldn't let him go. The possible miscarriage. But there was so much more he'd left out. Perhaps he shouldn't have. He loved Tonya, and keeping secrets wasn't a good way to start a relationship.

"I'm a nurse practitioner in this hospital. It's my job." Kathy folded her arms across her chest like a toddler digging her heels in, preparing for the argument. "I only want to offer my guidance."

"You're not medically responsible for our daughter," Victor said.

"And you don't have any say in her care." Kathy arched a brow. "Foster does and he wants—"

"No, I don't." Foster had enough. He wasn't going to stand there and let Kathy manipulate the situation like he'd done in the past. "There is no reason for you to be here other than to hurt us. To hurt me. Worse, to hurt Victoria, which is just sick and cruel." He curled his fingers around Kathy's biceps and guided her into the hallway. "I will call security, and I don't think you want me to do that in the hospital you work at."

Tonya followed. Foster wasn't sure how he felt about that, but he wasn't about to tell her to leave.

"I'm only trying to help you." Kathy yanked her arm free. "I wanted to know if there was anything I could do to make this transition easier, especially when you're taking her home. You shouldn't be doing that when she is so far along in the end-of-life process."

"This is none of your business and you are so full of shit and I can see it in your eyes. You're enjoying this." He raked his hand across the top of his head. He shouldn't have said that in front of Tonya, but it was time to end this insanity. One thing that bothered him about Kathy after his daughter died was that she never seemed to care about his loss. She only focused on the fact they could start a life together.

Something he couldn't even consider. Wouldn't consider.

"I can't believe you would think that of me. I don't understand why you always think the worst of me when all I've ever done is love and care for you. I still do, although sometimes I wish I didn't, but those feelings don't disappear when I've never had the chance to truly deal with our loss because you won't give me the chance."

"You're like a broken record with this."

"I have a question," Tonya said. "Does this have to do with the baby you claim you lost?"

"You've even got her brainwashed." Kathy pointed at Tonya.

"I just learned of this in the pharmacy a little bit

ago and I don't appreciate the implication I can't think for myself. You don't even know me," Tonya said. "This family is going through a lot right now and we don't need you coming in here with your drama, bringing up the past, with all your bullshit. Leave us alone."

Kathy sneered. "Fine. I'll leave *him* alone, but only if you hear what I have to say." She stepped between him and the door, tilting her chin toward the ceiling. "Ever since Lisa died, you've treated me as if I'm the enemy. You've never given me the opportunity to express my emotions about what happened."

Over the top of her head, he could see Victor inch closer.

Foster shook his head. The last thing he needed was for Victoria's parents to take a front row seat to this shitshow, again.

"You made your feelings very clear." Foster reached for Tonya's hand and laced his fingers through hers. It might have been a dick move, but he was so tired of the same fight.

"I gave you everything. My heart. My soul. I was there for you when Victoria wasn't. I'm still putting myself out there for you." She looked Tonya up and down. "And you throw your new girlfriend in my face. She should know the kind of man she's with."

Foster sucked in a deep breath. This wasn't going to end well.

"Trust me. I know who Foster is and I don't need you telling me." Tonya leaned into his body.

"Oh, really. Did he tell you about how I lost our child and he didn't care enough to come hold my hand?" she said, so loud the entire wing of the hospital could hear. She glanced over her shoulder. "He was too busy coddling his ex-wife."

There were only two people—no, three people—Kathy wanted to hear those words.

"This is a waste of all our time and energy. We're done," Foster said.

"We created a child that night and you'd like to pretend it never existed. I need you to acknowledge our baby. What we went through. I don't think that's too much to ask."

"You are some piece of work." Victor stomped into the hallway, closing the curtain. "When Foster asked you to prove to him that you were pregnant, you chose not to. You wouldn't even show him a pregnancy test. How can you expect him to grieve something he doesn't believe? And what's even worse, bringing it outside of the room where the mother of his late child is dying."

"I shouldn't have to prove anything," Kathy said. "How can I be expected to have closure when no one will respect me enough to even try to understand what this has been like for me?"

"Are you seriously going to ignore what's

happening right now?" Tonya took two small steps forward.

Foster tugged at her hand, but she didn't budge.

"This is not the time or the place. Leave," Tonya said.

"I hope you bought the morning after pill because the two of you don't deserve to be parents." Kathy turned on her heel and stormed off.

"Jesus, that woman gets under my skin." Victor sighed.

"I'm sorry you had to be witness to all of that, again." Foster rubbed his temple.

"Hopefully that's the last of her we'll ever have to see," Victor said. "Tonya, could you give Foster and me a minute?"

"Sure." Tonya squeezed Foster's hand. "I'll see if I can find that nurse with the discharge papers. I'll be right back."

Exhaustion took over Foster's mind and body. "I can't believe she's still pulling shit like this."

"She doesn't like us because I forced her hand and we all know she wasn't pregnant. It was a ruse to try to keep you, and having my office draw up a paternity test request sent her over the edge."

"I'm sure it did." Foster leaned against the wall. "I can't keep rehashing this."

"I didn't send Tonya away to talk about Kathy, but I do want to address something she said."

"And what's that?"

"I know what the morning after pill is and why on earth would you ever consider it when you and Tonya are such a beautiful couple? It's obvious how much the two of you love each other. Why would you try to prevent it, unless she doesn't want to have children?"

There are so many conversations Foster didn't want to have with others. However, his life had taken a complete one-eighty and outside of the fact that Victor and Denise struggled with how he handled their daughter, they had always been family. "Romantically, we've technically only been together for like two weeks."

"At least you're not denying that you love her."

"Loving her isn't the problem. That's the easy part. But we've both kept each other at arm's length for a long time."

"Because of Victoria?"

"No. Because of me," Foster admitted. "I've used the way in which Lisa died as an excuse not to live."

"Tell me something I don't know." Victor turned his head, peeking behind the curtain. "Look. I've always known you to be ridiculously responsible. I can't imagine you forgot birth control. Or that it just slipped your mind. If it did, subconsciously, you wanted it to."

"That sounds like something my therapist would say." Frankly, Foster had been thinking a lot about why he'd been so reckless. They'd had sex the night before, and he'd reached for a condom.

Just because they'd been in the kitchen meant jack shit.

"Truth be told, we haven't actually bought the Plan B pill." He nearly choked on the words and it wasn't because he was having this conversation with his ex-father-in-law, but because he didn't like the bitter taste the idea left in his mouth. "I don't know how I feel. I've been so adamant about not wanting to be in a relationship, get married, have a family, that having all this happen at once is making my head spin."

Victor rested his hand on Foster's shoulder and squeezed. "You have always been one of the kindest, gentlest, and strongest men I've ever met. I've admired your dedication and conviction—even though at times I haven't agreed with it—to my daughter."

"You always thought it was misguided."

"I still do because I believed it could be pointed in the direction of someone like Tonya. Maybe you needed to do that until you and Tonya were ready to take the giant leap, but I wish you would reconsider having a family."

"Thank you. Your support means a lot."

"Denise and I will always be here for you. Always. We've never wanted you out of our lives." Victor dabbed his eyes. "And when Victoria passes, we'll still want to have a relationship with you. If you have more children, we hope that you'll bring them around and let us get to know them. We love you like you're our own son."

A guttural sob filled his throat. He tried to swallow it, but he couldn't. He inhaled slowly. "We better get back inside Victoria's room." He pulled himself together. Once he was alone with Tonya, he'd have another conversation about what to do next.

17

*F*oster sat at the edge of his bed and sighed. A combination of sadness and anger filled his soul.

Victoria was gone.

He hadn't even been able to bring her back to his place. She died forty minutes after the altercation with Kathy. There were then hours of decision-making and paperwork.

Thank God for Tonya. She'd been his rock. He had no idea what he would have done had she not been by his side. But his heart still broke into a million pieces.

He tried to tell himself that Victoria was in a better place. That maybe she'd been released of all her addictions and she'd been reunited with their daughter.

He gripped the side of the mattress. His soul

JEN TALTY

ached. His heart filled with a mixture of pain and rage. The urge to disappear into the fabric of the mountains behind his house hadn't been as prevalent as when Victoria was released from prison. He'd told himself all these years that he could forgive her for what she'd done because she'd been living in the grips of her drug use. His brain understood that Victoria had never been in her right mind. If she had, she would have never chosen a fix over their precious little girl.

By the time they'd gotten home, it was early the next morning, and he and Tonya had spent all of Sunday in bed.

The bathroom door opened, and Tonya stepped out into the loft. Her hair was perfectly styled, and her makeup was applied for the day. She stole his breath. She was his world and he never wanted to let her go.

Ever.

She was his compass, just like Doug had described.

"I only have one meeting today." She sat down next to him, running her hands up and down his back. "I can cancel if you want me to."

He took her hand, and all his negative feelings disappeared. "There's no reason for you to do that."

Foster ran a hand over his face. Victor and Denise didn't want to have a funeral, or even a celebration of life. Technically, it was no longer their decision. Even though Foster and Victoria were divorced, she'd signed over everything to him, but she hadn't wanted any service either. She had one request and that was to have her ashes scattered over their daughter's grave. He'd checked with the cemetery and they'd confirmed they'd be able to grant that wish.

There would be no ceremony. Just him and Victoria's parents, but he wasn't ready to do it yet and Victor told him to take his time.

His cell dinged. He lifted it and stared at the calendar reminder.

Fuck.

He needed to leave in ten minutes to go pick up Maxwell and take him to the doctor.

He understood why Maxwell didn't want to fight. He was an old man who'd lived a good, decent, kind life. Since Foster lost his daughter, he lived on the fringe of existence. He woke up every day and did what was expected on the surface. He ate food. He smiled and acknowledged others. He worked. However, at the end of the day, it was as if he shut off his soul and blended into the background like leaves rustling in the wind.

Since allowing Tonya completely into his heart, he could no longer comprehend why Maxwell didn't want his family around.

"I wanted to stop by my grandpa's place and see how he is doing. Can you come with me?" Tonya asked.

"Why don't I meet you there." Foster was going to

have to have a major heart-to-heart with Maxwell. "I have some errands to run."

"Are you sure? I don't mind coming back." She cupped his face. "You tossed and turned all night. I'm worried about you."

He took her chin with his thumb and forefinger. "I love you," he whispered. "I'm going to be fine."

"I love you too. But—"

He cut off her words with a passionate kiss. "My sleepless night had nothing to do with Victoria." He'd avoided this conversation since Victoria's death because it didn't feel right. When they'd made love at six in the morning and she'd reached for the condoms, he obliged, but he hadn't wanted to use them. Not because he didn't like them, though that was true, but because he wanted the world with Tonya. They loved each other. They also knew each other better than most couples. He knew that to be a fact. They might have only been romantically involved for a few short weeks, but they'd loved each other for a long time. She was his north star. His way home. "How do you feel about not taking that damn pill?"

She tilted her head. "That's playing an interesting game with our lives."

"It's no game," he said. "Perhaps I'm crazy. Maybe being in love for the first time at my age has affected my judgment, but I don't want to spend another second of my life without you in it and the idea of having a family with you—of being part of a family with you—makes me feel things I never thought were possible again."

A tear rolled down her cheek.

"Shit. I didn't mean to make you cry."

"I'm not sad. I might be in shock."

He chuckled. "If things don't work out this time, maybe we will wait a little bit, but I want to get married and I think having a couple little mini-mes would be cool."

"Is that a proposal?"

"It's not a very good one, is it?"

She palmed his cheek. "For us, it's perfect. Only, you'll have to pick someone to be the wedding driver for us because, while I don't want a wedding other than with my family present, I want that boat ride."

"Oh, I'm the only one who can be your wedding driver." He kissed her, hard. "I'll see you at your grandfather's after your appointment." He stood, lifting her off the bed.

She patted the center of his chest. "Text me when you're on your way."

"Will do." He watched her stroll toward the staircase. She glanced over her shoulder and smiled, blowing him a kiss.

His heart dropped to the center of his gut.

Her grandfather was going to tell his family the truth of his illness today.

Or he was.

Foster set the glass of water on the table in front of Maxwell before sitting down with a soda for himself. He glanced at his cell. Tonya was ten minutes away.

"Victoria's death has really affected you deeply." Maxwell took the glass with a shaky hand, lifting it to his lips. The doctor's visit had been eye-opening for Foster because he understood the depth of Maxwell's illness.

Inoperable.

Terminal.

At most, three months.

"To be honest, I'm more relieved than anything else. I know that makes me sound like a jerk."

"You weren't responsible for her," Maxwell said. "You did everything humanly possible to protect Victoria. Don't be too hard on yourself."

"I'm ready to move on with my life. With Tonya. We talked about getting married today."

"No way. That's fast."

"We love each other."

"I've known that for a long time," Maxwell said. "But why are you so serious if that's the case? This should be a time of light and joy."

"Because I won't lie to her." Foster arched a brow.

Maxwell narrowed his stare. "What does that mean?"

"I can't keep your secret. Not from her. Not from

the rest of your family. It's no way to start a new life. She'll be here shortly. You can tell her and work through the rest of the family."

Maxwell set the glass on the table a little harshly. The water sloshed over the sides and onto his hand. "What right do you have to dictate how I deal with my cancer? I trusted you, and you're going to betray me like this? How dare you."

"How dare me? You put me in an impossible position. Worse, you used my lack of a relationship with your granddaughter to get me to keep your secret from your entire family, and that's not fair to me, you, or to them. They love you, and while I totally understand you don't want to burden them, can you accept that they will feel completely and utterly betrayed by you when they find out you kept this from them? Not to mention how it will affect my relationship moving forward."

"They are going to want me to fight. I don't have any left in me. Besides, you heard the doctor; even with treatment, I don't have much time left. I don't want it to be with sad faces."

"You're not giving them enough credit." Foster sipped his beer. "You and I both know what it's like to have a child ripped from our world long before we're ready. But we also know that no one is ever really ready to deal with loss. It always hurts, and it's messy. But I know Tonya, and if she was sitting with you at that appointment today, holding your hand, she would have hugged you and accepted that your days are numbered, because no offense, old man, you're not getting any younger anyway."

Maxwell poked Foster in the arm. "That's just wrong." He laughed. "But I am eighty-something. I've had a good life. Knowing that you and Tonya have finally found each other makes me happy." Maxwell swiped his cheeks. "How did you go from being broken up to having the marriage talk?"

Foster's entire life flashed like a movie in fast-forward. Growing up, he'd been a little on the wild side. His parents were constantly having to take away his toys and later the keys to the car. But he had to grow up fast when Lisa came along. He hadn't thought twice about it. He never once regretted his decision to marry Victoria. Not even when things got bad.

Truth be told, his dissatisfaction in his marriage had been survivable because of Lisa.

The loss of his precious child came crushing down on his chest, squeezing his heart with a death grip. His breathing became labored. It always felt as though he were going to die. It was a sensation he'd grown used to. It took time for it to pass; however, lately it disappeared in seconds.

Tonya.

Her love filled his soul like smooth whiskey. It didn't replace his pain, but it soothed it in such a way that allowed him to step from the past into the present. It was as if his little girl was telling him it was time.

"This might sound strange, but it's like for the last few months we've been dating. We were always together. Sometimes we'd watch movies. Or she'd help me with Victoria. We had dinner together. I knew if either one of us ever told the other how we felt, there was no going back, so I kept the genie in the bottle. I dug my heels in when Tonya let him out because I was scared of how much I loved her and what that meant."

Maxwell sniffled. "When do you plan on marrying my grandbaby?"

"I don't know. That's really up to Tonya. I feel like at this point I'm along for the ride."

"Good answer." Maxwell took in a long, slow breath. "Except I need you do this old man a favor."

Foster tilted his head. "Favors right now are in short supply until you come clean."

"I will. I promise. But I want to see the two of you get married before I die."

18

THREE WEEKS LATER...

"...*Y*ou may kiss your bride."

The words hung in the air as Foster pulled Tonya closer and pressed his mouth over her lips.

The few people in attendance clapped and cheered. Music from the Blue Moon restaurant tickled her ears and a few shouts from the patrons made their way down to the docks while her stomach filled with butterflies.

She was married.

To Foster.

The wedding driver was going to take her for a ride around the bay on her wedding day. She wasn't going to stand on the dock and watch him take some other bride.

It was her turn.

A fairy tale.

She had everything she had ever dreamed about.

And her grandfather had been able to attend.

"Hello, wife," Foster whispered.

"I honestly never thought I'd hear those words come out of your mouth." She palmed his cheek. "It's music to my ears."

"I love you."

"I love you right back." She turned and faced her family, along with Foster's mother, Victor, and Denise. At first, Foster thought it might feel weird or that they wouldn't want to be there, but in the end, they were still part of his family. She was happy to embrace them.

Her father was the first to race to her side and hug her. Tears filled her eyes and she smiled at her grandfather. His health continued to decline. It wouldn't be long now.

"That was a beautiful ceremony," her father said.

"Thanks, Daddy." She kissed his cheek and made her way to her grandpa. "How are you doing?" She knelt at his side, taking his frail, pale hand.

"I've never been happier," he said. "All my grandbabies are married. Two of them are pregnant and I know your turn will come soon enough."

She and Foster had decided they needed a little more time to get used to how quickly their lives had changed before breaking their even bigger news, which is why they had decided to get married on the docks, leave on the boat for their honeymoon camping trip, and let everyone else party at the Blue Moon restaurant. That way they didn't have to explain why she wasn't drinking.

But she couldn't keep it a secret from her grandfather.

She glanced over her shoulder and waved to her new husband.

"Hey, old man," Foster said as he strolled across the wood planks. "Doesn't my wife look amazing?"

"I bet he says that at least twenty times before the day is done," her grandfather said. He held out his arms. "Help me to my feet."

Foster leaned forward. "I can't get her to call me husband."

She laughed. "If you beg me, I might."

"My innocent ears," her grandfather said. "How long will the two of you be gone?"

"Two nights." Foster held her grandpa up. "It's still major wedding season and we both have a lot of work."

"As you know, I moved into my son's house," her grandpa said. "My house is now empty and I want to keep it in the family. I want the two of you to have it. Consider it my wedding gift." He waved a shaky hand. "I know that Foster has a house and he's renovating it, but—"

"If Tonya wants to live there, then I'd be honored." Foster smiled. "It's a beautiful home."

"And a great place to raise a family," she added,

tilting her head, staring at Foster, willing him to understand her wishes.

He nodded. "You can tell him."

"Tell me what?"

"We didn't tell anyone in part because we didn't want to take away from Tiki or Tayla, but also because there's been a lot going on in our lives."

Her grandfather grabbed her arm. "Are you going to have a baby too?"

"Yes, Grandpa." Her heart filled with so much love she thought it might burst.

"You're going to make great parents together," her grandfather said. "I don't know when I've ever felt this much joy. It's so wonderful to come to the end of the road in life and know that the people you love the most have found their people and their happy place."

"I love you, Grandpa." She kissed his cheek. "We'll see you when we get back."

Foster helped him up the step where Gael and Lake took over, leading him up the stairs and into the party.

"Are you ready to go on your wedding boat ride?" Foster lifted his arm.

"Oh hell, yes." She looped her hand through his arm. "Who would have thought the wedding driver would turn out to be my husband."

19

TWO WEEKS LATER...

*T*onya stood at the graveside with her two sisters. She stared at the casket that held her grandfather. Tears burned her eyes. "I can't believe he's gone."

"It's like as soon as he knew we were all pregnant, he let go." Tayla dabbed her eyes.

"I can't believe we're all due within five days of each other," Tiki said. "How the hell does that happen?"

Tonya leaned forward and rested her rose on top of the wood box. "If Grandpa were here, he'd say something like, *do you need a lesson in the birds and the bees because I can give you one.*"

"I going to miss him." Tiki placed her flower over Tonya's.

"Who gets the name Maxwell?" Tayla asked.

"Whoever has a boy first," Tonya said. "Or if we

all have boys, maybe we all use it as a middle name. Although Foster doesn't want to find out the sex."

"Gael is dying to know," Tayla said.

"So is Lake." Tiki took Tonya's hand. "If we have girls, we go with Maxine."

"I'm sure we can come up with all sorts of fun names that will honor Maxwell James Johnson." Tonya looped her free arm around Tayla.

They walked down the path toward their husbands.

Where one life ended, another one began.

Another saying her grandfather used to tell her and in this case, it was three and she completely believed it.

"I'll see you all back at Mom and Dad's." She paused about ten paces from Foster, giving each of her sisters a quick hug.

Foster strolled in her direction. "How are you holding up?" he asked.

"I'm okay." She sighed. "How are you?"

"It brings up a lot," he admitted. "We've had a lot of loss mixed with so much good." He placed his hand on the small of her back. "I often feel guilty for being so damn happy."

"I do too."

"We don't have to do this today," Foster said softly.

"No. My grandfather is smiling down on us. He'd take this as an honor." She swallowed a guttural sob when Denise and Victor came into view.

They stood over Lisa's graveside, holding what had to be Victoria's urn.

Foster slowed his pace. "I thought I'd forgiven her," he whispered. Every muscle in his body tensed. His blood went cold. He couldn't swallow.

"It's okay to be angry," Tonya said.

He held back his snippy response because it wouldn't be fair to take anything out on the one woman who had stood by him through some of the toughest times in his life. Instead, he took in a deep calming breath and tried to clear his mind of the past. He didn't live there anymore. He chose the present and the future he had with Tonya.

Nothing he did would ever bring back Lisa. The only way to truly honor her memory was to be the kind of man that would make her proud.

And that would be to let go of Victoria and all the pain and misery that part of his life had brought.

"I don't want to be mad at her anymore." He sighed. "I'm tired of this constantly coming back."

"What would my grandfather say?"

Foster chuckled. There were a dozen sayings he could come up with. "Shit or get off the pot. You can't move forward if you have two feet stuck in the past. But I think my favorite one that comes to mind is, stop being such an asshole and just do what needs

doing, like changing my lightbulb in the guest room."
He nudged Tonya forward. "Let's do this."

A thickness filled his throat as he approached his
daughter's grave. She would have been fifteen years
old. Her next birthday she would have been begging
him for her permit.

He'd never have the opportunity to chase off boys.
Or to walk her down the aisle. All those firsts were
ripped from him in an instant.

But he couldn't hang on to the rage in his heart
anymore. Not because he found love. Or because he
had a new baby on the way. Or even because Victoria
had passed. He had to let it go because an old man
taught him that living life meant honoring those we
loved.

And he loved his little girl with every fiber of his
being.

"Thanks for coming," Foster said.

"Tonya, we are so sorry for your loss." Victor
curled his fingers around her biceps. "Your grandfather, while we didn't know him well, was so kind to us
at your wedding."

"He was a good man," Tonya said.

"We're surprised you picked today to do this."
Victor handed Foster the urn.

"My grandfather would have wanted it." Tonya
glanced up and smiled. "He believed in fresh starts
and I'm sure he's looking down on all of us, grateful
that we've been able to come together like this."

Foster ran his hand over the tombstone. "Is there anything either of you would like to say?"

Denise pulled out a handkerchief. "Foster." She grabbed his hand. "You have always been a shining light in our lives. I know that we spent a few years almost cutting you out."

"You did what you needed to do," Foster said. "I never felt like you didn't care for me during that time. I honestly understood."

"This is why we want to be a part of your life now," Victor added. "Tonya. We know we have no right to ask this of you, especially here, now. However, as we bring our daughter together with our granddaughter, we'd like to give you this." Victor stuck his hand into his coat pocket. "This was my father's and it would have gone to Lisa."

Foster swallowed.

Hard.

"The compass," he whispered.

"Yes. It might seem silly, but it's been handed down from one generation to the next," Denise said. "We know your baby isn't our family. However, we've always felt as though Foster is and we want your child to have it."

Foster took the compass between his fingers. His hand shook. This very object sat next to Lisa's bed a long time ago. She'd kiss it every night before she closed her eyes. She'd never met her great-grandfather. He'd passed long before she was born. But she loved the damn compass. "We can't accept this."

Tonya laid her soft hands over his and his heart melted into a million pieces. Not only did he know he had to take the compass, but he accepted he wanted it.

"That's such an amazing gift," Tonya said. "Will you give us a moment?"

"Sure." Victor took his wife's hand and strolled toward the big oak tree twenty feet away.

"What's going on?" Foster asked.

"My sisters and I were talking about all the various godparent scenarios and we were giving ourselves headaches trying to figure it out. But this solves the problem."

"I don't follow."

"Lake and Tiki can be godparents to Gael and Tayla's baby, and then Gael and Tayla can be godparents to Lake and Tiki's kid. We can ask Denise and Victor to be the godparents of our baby." Tonya took Foster's hand and placed it over her stomach. It was still flat, but he knew his baby grew inside.

His knees grew weak. His vision blurred. "Are you sure you want to do that? It takes it outside of family."

"No, it doesn't. They are *your* family. That means they are mine too and our baby's," she said. "They have no other children. They will never have more grandchildren. My grandpa always told me that he could get through the days easier because of my dad and us. He had so much to live for, especially after my grandma died."

Foster could actually relate to that statement. He cupped her face and brushed his lips over her mouth. "You are the most amazing person I've ever met."

"You bring out the best in me."

A tear burned a path down his cheek. "Do you enjoy seeing me cry?"

"Actually, I hate it." She wiped it away. "But I might make you sob because if this kid is a boy, we should name him Maxwell Victor."

Foster dropped his head to hers and closed his eyes. "You are my compass and I will love you with all of my heart forever. You can count on that."

EPILOGUE

*F*oster lifted his son and cradled him to his chest.

Maxwell Victor Landon.

The only boy.

Tayla had a girl seven days ago which she named Maxie Marie Waylon. Tiki named her little girl, Maddie Maxine Grant, who was born five days ago.

All tributes to their grandfather.

Only Foster's child had so many other little hidden meanings. He kissed Maxwell's forehead and inhaled that wonderful baby scent that reminded him what it meant to be alive. There were moments he worried that his son carried too many burdens. Too many memories attached to his existence.

A sister he'd never really know except for stories.

Godparents who loved him as if they were grandparents.

A great grandfather for which he was named after.

And his half sister's mother who would always be part of Foster's existence. A fact he'd finally accepted.

"Are you going to stand there hogging him, or are you going to let his mother have him?"

Foster sighed and blinked. "He's too perfect." He placed him on Tonya's stomach. Her delivery had been easy-ish. Tonya had a plan and she was determined to follow it. When things didn't go her way, she shifted gears and was a real trooper. Foster was, as always, along for the ride.

"I can't get over how much he looks like you," Tonya said.

"That's why he's perfect." Foster sat on the edge of bed, putting his finger in Maxwell's hand. "But I see some of your grandpa in him."

"You're just saying that."

"No. Look at his nose. That's your grandfather all the way."

Tonya laughed. "My poor parents. They are so worried we're all going to want to travel or go on a cruise together and leave three same-aged grandkids with them."

"I'll be down for that in a few years." He leaned over and kissed his beautiful wife's temple. "But we do have Denise and Victor we can call upon. They are good with babies."

"That we do." She glanced up. "You are my compass."

"And you are mine."

ABOUT THE AUTHOR

Jen Talty is the *USA Today* Bestselling Author of Contemporary Romance, Romantic Suspense, and Paranormal Romance. In the fall of 2020, her short story was selected and featured in a 1001 Dark Nights Anthology.

Regardless of the genre, her goal is to take you on a ride that will leave you floating under the sun with warmth in your heart. She writes stories about broken heroes and heroines who aren't necessarily looking for romance, but in the end, they find the kind of love books are written about :).

She first started writing while carting her kids to one hockey rink after the other, averaging 170 games per year between 3 kids in 2 countries and 5 states. Her first book, IN TWO WEEKS was originally published in 2007. In 2010 she helped form a publishing company (Cool Gus Publishing) with *NY Times* Bestselling Author Bob Mayer where she ran the technical side of the business through 2016.

Jen is currently enjoying the next phase of her life… the empty nester! She and her husband reside in Jupiter, Florida.

Grab a glass of vino, kick back, relax, and let the romance roll in…

Sign up for my Newsletter (https://dl.bookfunnel.com/ 82gm8b9k4y) where I often give away free books before publication.

Join my private Facebook group (https://www.facebook.com/ groups/191706547909047/) where I post exclusive excerpts and discuss all things murder and love!

Never miss a new release. Follow me on Amazon:amazon.com/author/jentalty

And on Bookbub: bookbub.com/authors/jen-talty

ALSO BY JEN TALTY

Brand new series: SAFE HARBOR!

MINE TO KEEP

MINE TO SAVE

MINE TO PROTECT

Check out LOVE IN THE ADIRONDACKS!

SHATTERED DREAMS

AN INCONVENIENT FLAME

THE WEDDING DRIVER

NY STATE TROOPER SERIES (also set in the Adirondacks!)

In Two Weeks

Dark Water

Deadly Secrets

Murder in Paradise Bay

To Protect His own

Deadly Seduction

When A Stranger Calls

His Deadly Past

The Corkscrew Killer

Brand New Novella for the First Responders series

A spin-off from the NY State Troopers series

PLAYING WITH FIRE

PRIVATE CONVERSATION

THE RIGHT GROOM

AFTER THE FIRE

CAUGHT IN THE FLAMES

CHASING THE FIRE

Legacy Series

Dark Legacy

Legacy of Lies

Secret Legacy

Emerald City

INVESTIGATE AWAY

SAIL AWAY

Colorado Brotherhood Protectors

Fighting For Esme

Defending Raven

Fay's Six

Yellowstone Brotherhood Protectors

Guarding Payton

Candlewood Falls

RIVERS EDGE

THE BURIED SECRET

ITS IN HIS KISS

LIPS OF AN ANGEL

It's all in the Whiskey

JOHNNIE WALKER

GEORGIA MOON

JACK DANIELS

JIM BEAM

WHISKEY SOUR

WHISKEY COBBLER

WHISKEY SMASH

IRISH WHISKEY

The Monroes

COLOR ME YOURS

COLOR ME SMART

COLOR ME FREE

COLOR ME LUCKY

COLOR ME ICE

COLOR ME HOME

Search and Rescue

PROTECTING AINSLEY

PROTECTING CLOVER

PROTECTING OLYMPIA

PROTECTING FREEDOM

PROTECTING PRINCESS

PROTECTING MARLOWE

DELTA FORCE-NEXT GENERATION

SHIELDING JOLENE

SHIELDING AALYIAH

SHIELDING LAINE

SHIELDING TALULLAH

SHIELDING MARIBEL

The Men of Thief Lake

REKINDLED

DESTINY'S DREAM

Federal Investigators

JANE DOE'S RETURN

THE BUTTERFLY MURDERS

THE AEGIS NETWORK

The Sarich Brother

THE LIGHTHOUSE

HER LAST HOPE

THE LAST FLIGHT

THE RETURN HOME

THE MATRIARCH

More Aegis Network

MAX & MILIAN

A CHRISTMAS MIRACLE

SPINNING WHEELS

HOLIDAY'S VACATION

Special Forces Operation Alpha

BURNING DESIRE

BURNING KISS

BURNING SKIES

BURNING LIES

BURNING HEART

BURNING BED

REMEMBER ME ALWAYS

The Brotherhood Protectors

Out of the Wild

ROUGH JUSTICE

ROUGH AROUND THE EDGES

ROUGH RIDE

ROUGH EDGE

ROUGH BEAUTY

The Brotherhood Protectors

The Saving Series

SAVING LOVE

SAVING MAGNOLIA

SAVING LEATHER

Hot Hunks

Cove's Blind Date Blows Up

My Everyday Hero – Ledger

Tempting Tavor

Malachi's Mystic Assignment

Needing Neor

Holiday Romances

A CHRISTMAS GETAWAY

ALASKAN CHRISTMAS

WHISPERS

CHRISTMAS IN THE SAND

Heroes & Heroines on the Field

TAKING A RISK

TEE TIME

A New Dawn

THE BLIND DATE

SPRING FLING

SUMMERS GONE

WINTER WEDDING

THE AWAKENING

The Collective Order

THE LOST SISTER

THE LOST SOLDIER

THE LOST SOUL

THE LOST CONNECTION

THE NEW ORDER